'Look,' Alex said. 'I won't pretend I'm madly in love with you or anything like that, but, as I see it, there are advantages to both of us in getting married.'

A thrill of sadness went through Judy at his easy dismissal of love, but she tried to match his casual tone. 'Such as?' she asked jauntily.

'Well, in the first place there's Robin. He needs a father and I want to be with him. Maybe I wouldn't have wound up with you if things had been different, but I'm thirty-two years old and I'm ready to settle down. You've already had my son, so marrying you seems like the obvious thing to do. I can see from this place that you know how to run a house, and Kate says you're a great cook. And even if you're not ravishingly beautiful, you're quite pretty. You'll do me, anyway.'

'Thank you,' said Judy in a dangerous voice. 'How kind of you, lord and master. So, if I understand correctly, what you get out of this little marriage of convenience is unlimited access to your son, free housekeeping, meals on the table, and the sexual gratification of a wife who is just about pretty enough to measure up to your exacting standards. And what exactly do I get? Piles of dirty dishes, the privilege of ironing your shirts, and free plastic surgery if my looks turn out not to be quite up to par?'

Angela Devine was born in Tasmania and took a Ph.D in Classics. After several years as a university lecturer in New South Wales, she returned to Tasmania to try her hand at writing. With a hospital plot in mind, she pounced on several medical friends for the necessary background. Fortunately her next door neighbour is a surgeon, who kindly performed many operations into her tape recorder. The resulting book is her first Medical Romance, *Family Matters*.

She is married to an American marine biologist and has four children. Her interests are sailing, archaelogy and classical music.

FAMILY MATTERS

BY

ANGELA DEVINE

MILLS & BOON LIMITED
ETON HOUSE   18-24 PARADISE ROAD
RICHMOND   SURREY   TW9 1SR

First published in Great Britain 1990
by Mills & Boon Limited

© Angela Devine 1990

Australian copyright 1990
Philippine copyright 1990
This edition 1990

ISBN 0 263 76758 2

Set in Times 10 on 10½ pt.
03 – 9003 – 61804

Typeset in Great Britain by The Picador Group, Bristol

Made and Printed in Great Britain

CHAPTER ONE

SHE heard it over the hospital loudspeaker. It was a simple enough announcement, but it dropped into Judy's quiet world with all the force of a bomb going off.

'Mr Alexander Shaw. Paging Mr Alexander Shaw. Could you report to Paediatrics, please, sir?'

Judy felt her heart thumping wildly. Alexander Shaw? Surely there couldn't be two Alexander Shaws involved in Paediatrics? But Alex was in Canada, not here in Australia. Her head in a whirl, she stepped into the lift and pressed the button for the sixth floor. She had to go to Paediatrics this morning anyway, so she might as well check for herself. Judy was not the sort of girl to duck an unpleasant situation.

He was leaning over a child's bed with his back turned to her when she entered the ward, but there could be no mistaking that lithe muscular body and the glossy dark hair. Judy gave an involuntary gasp. The matron, who was standing beside him, moved forward to greet her.

'Oh, Mr Shaw, I'd like you to meet one of our young interns, Dr Judith Lacey. Dr Lacey, this is Mr Alexander Shaw, the new consultant surgeon. He's just arrived from Canada.'

'How do you do?' said Alex, coming forward with his hand outstretched.

Judy felt the warm, firm pressure of his fingers and looked straight into his liquid brown eyes. A sudden frown creased his forehead as something about her tantalised his memory. His gaze travelled down over her shiny chestnut hair, her wistful face with the little sprinkle of freckles across the nose, and the quirky, humorous mouth. Her body, he noted with

5

disappointment, was hidden in an ugly lab coat, but her legs were slim and shapely.

'You look familiar,' he said. 'Do I know you from somewhere, Dr Lacey?'

Of course you do, Judy wanted to cry. You're the father of my child! But she merely turned her coolly appraising green eyes on him and nodded.

'Yes,' she said. 'I was at your party the night you won the Beattie Prize for Surgery. Just before you left for Canada.'

That went home. She saw the faint dark flush mount on his cheekbones under the olive skin.

'Oh, yes,' he said. 'So you were. I'm sorry I didn't recognise you sooner. You really haven't changed much.'

Oh, haven't I? thought Judy grimly, but she saw no point in arguing about it.

'I'm sorry to interrupt you, Matron, but could I just collect the X-rays for the Horne child? Professor Castle wants to see them,' she said.

As the matron turned away towards the nurse's desk, Alex spoke again. 'Dr Lacey?'

His voice was deep and throaty, just as she remembered it.

'Yes, Mr Shaw?'

'While you're here, perhaps you'd like to take a look at this child's cheek and tell me your diagnosis.'

Conscious of Alex's intent scrutiny, Judy moved forward and looked down at the little girl on the bed. There was a pink, cauliflower-shaped lump on the child's cheek and Judy almost breathed a sigh of relief. Carefully she examined the girl's cheek for associated lumps and then straightened up.

'I think it's a strawberry naevus,' she said.

'Good. And the treatment?'

'Excision,' replied Judy without hesitation.

'Good,' said Alex approvingly. 'Ah, here's Matron back with your X-rays.'

As she left with the yellow envelope, Judy could feel Alex's gaze raking her skin. She wondered if he could see her legs shaking, but she kept her head high and remained outwardly calm until she was out of sight. Only when she was safely out of the ward did she give vent for a brief moment to her feelings. Blinded by a sudden mist of tears, she blundered into a staff washroom and let herself go. Dropping the X-rays on a handy chair, she covered her face and gave a long, choking gasp.

'Alex Shaw,' she murmured in a muffled voice. 'Alex Shaw! I just don't believe it. How on earth am I going to cope?' Dashing away the tears with the back of her hand, she glared fiercely at herself in the mirror. Her pale, tear-stained face glared back at her. 'You'll cope the way you've always coped,' she told herself urgently. 'Nobody needs to know that Alex is Robin's father, least of all Alex. Now just play it cool and get on with the job!'

She was acutely conscious that the door might open at any moment, and she had no wish to be found weeping into the washbasin, so she splashed her face with cold water and dabbed it resolutely with a paper towel. Then, picking up the envelope again, she strode off towards the lift. As it shuddered down the building, she leant back against its yellow vinyl wall and sighed.

It was finished, she thought bitterly. Finished. That brief fling with Alex almost five years ago that had led to so much heartache for her. An unwanted pregnancy, blazing rows with her family, whisperings in the hospital corridors that stopped as soon as she approached. And that gruelling fight to keep going, to keep her baby, to complete her training. Well, she had done it in the end. Had stuck doggedly to her determination not to reveal the identity of Robin's father, not to let any well-meaning busybodies inform him of her plight. The only person Judy had confided in was her best friend Kate Wilson, and Kate had always remained loyally silent in spite of her belief that Alex should be told the truth. But in the end Alex had gone to Canada in ignorance, and married his fiancée without ever having to think twice about Judy. But surely in return she was entitled to a bit of peace? A chance to let old wounds heal and forget the past?

The trouble was, she reflected grimly, that the old wounds felt as fresh as ever. Walking into that ward had been like going back over four years. The mere sight of Alex had triggered the same quickening in her pulse, the same sense of aching need as she had felt when she was twenty. How could she bear it, if she had to see him every day? Well, you won't have to, she told herself severely. You're on Casualty, not Theatre. Most of your patients are adults. And next week you'll be transferring to Geriatrics, and you certainly won't see him there! All you have to do is survive the next week. What can happen in a week?

The lift opened and she stepped out on the ground floor. Casualty was in its usual state of frantic overwork, and she was barely inside the door before she found herself stitching a chisel wound in a carpenter's hand. After that there was a suspected appendicitis case to examine, a toddler who had swallowed half a clothes peg, an elderly woman having an asthma attack and a motorist with burns from a carelessly removed radiator cap. All comforting routine cases, which were straightforward enough to handle, but kept her too busy to brood. Judy heaved a mental sigh of relief and began to relax. But then, in the afternoon, a patient appeared who destroyed her fragile calm.

She returned from lunch to find a nine-year-old boy groaning and writhing on a couch in one of the cubicles with his anxious mother hovering next to him.

'Hello,' said Judy, coming forward. 'I'm Dr Lacey. Can I help you?'

'Oh, Doctor. Thank heavens you're here. Michael's

having these terrible pains in his side and I've no idea what's the matter with him.'

Judy sat down beside the child and winked at him. She was encouraged to see that, in spite of his pain, he managed to wink back. He reminded her a little of her son Robin, with his dark hair and limpid eyes, and she felt a rush of sympathy for his mother.

'OK, Michael, let's take a look at you,' she said.

As her fingers probed expertly over the child's flank, she questioned his mother closely. How long had he been feeling pain? Had it happened before? Was the pain very severe? Did it seem to get worse as time went on? Did he always grip his right side when the pain was at its worst? Did he suffer pain on passing urine? Added together, the answers formed an ominous picture and Judy was not surprised when she found a large mass palpable in the abdomen. Almost certainly a kidney tumour, she thought in dismay. But her face remained professionally calm as she helped Michael put on his shirt.

'Mrs Burrows, I'd like to admit Michael and have him examined by our paediatric surgeon,' said Judy.

As she expected, a flood of panic-stricken questions followed, but she reassured the woman as well as she could and, after giving the child an injection of thirty milligrams of pethidine, went off to phone Alex.

'Mr Shaw? Judith Lacey here. I'm calling from Casualty at St Thomas's. I've got a nine-year-old boy here with a suspected kidney tumour. I'd like you to examine him as soon as possible.'

'I'm pretty tied up at the moment in my consulting rooms,' said Alex. 'But I'll be over as soon as I can.'

It was after five-thirty when he finally arrived, and Judy could have packed up and gone home, but something made her stay. She told herself it was only concern for Michael, but deep down she knew it was more than that. Although she might despise herself for it, the truth was that she was hungry for another glimpse of Alex. As she watched him leaning over the dark-haired boy in the bed, a little pang went through her. What a pity it was that Alex would never lean over Robin like that, never even know of his son's existence! Alex's long, sensitive fingers finished their examination and he ruffled the boy's hair.

'All right, tiger,' he said gently. 'That's it for now. Dr Lacey, may I see you for a moment in Sister's office?'

She looked at him fearfully as he led her into the room and shut the door.

'Is it a kidney tumour?' she asked.

'Yes, almost certainly' agreed Alex. 'The real question now is just how far it's spread. I'll put him down for tests next Thursday. If we're lucky, we may be able to remove it all then, but I've a nasty suspicion it may have become attached to a major blood-vessel. If that's so, he'll have to go to Melbourne for major surgery.'

'Poor kid,' said Judy, and was horrified to hear the tremor in her own voice.

'What is it?' asked Alex sharply. 'Is he someone you know?'

Judy shook her head wordlessly. No. He just reminds me of my son, she thought. Our son.

'Then you'd better cultivate detachment,' advised Alex crisply. 'The last thing you can afford to do is get emotionally involved.'

That warning was still ringing in Judy's ears when she went to collect Robin from the babysitter's. Oh, Alex had been talking about a patient, had never intended any irony or double meaning. But his advice was amazingly apt for their own situation. The trouble was that Judy simply couldn't follow it, couldn't cultivate detachment where Alex was concerned. And, like it or not, she was still emotionally involved with Alex up to her neck.

The moment Kate Wilson opened the front door, she saw that something was wrong. Judy was as pale as a sheet of paper, and she looked dazed.

'Judy! Whatever is it? Did one of your patients die?'

'No, nothing like that,' said Judy, desperately shaking her head. 'It's—I . . . '

To her horror and amazement, she found that tears were running down her face and spilling all over her coat.

'Come in,' said Kate in distress, putting her arms around Judy and pulling her into the hall. 'Sit down and I'll make you some coffee, and you can tell me all about it.'

'Where's Robin?' choked Judy, fighting for control.

'Still asleep. Now don't say anything until you've had something hot to drink.'

Judy sat at the table twisting her fingers together, while Kate fussed with the coffee percolator in the tiny kitchen. Although small, it was a cosy house with a dazzling view of the River Derwent below. Judy's own flat downstairs was tucked into the slope of the block and had an equally dazzling view. After bad days at the hospital, she often sat in her living-room until late at night watching the lights of the ships. But now she was too upset even to find consolation in the beauty of the water.

'There,' said Kate, setting down a tray in front of her. 'Hot and sweet, just the way you like it. Now drink up and then tell Aunt Kate all about it.'

Judy took a gulp of the coffee and felt herself grow calmer. She drew in a deep breath. 'Alex is back,' she said.

'Alex?' echoed Kate in disbelief. 'Back where? In Australia?'

'Not just Australia,' said Judy with a choking laugh. 'Right here in Hobart at St Thomas's Hospital.'

'Have you seen him?'

'Yes,' said Judy wearily. 'I ran into him on the wards this morning. He didn't even recognise me. Well, not at first anyway.'

Kate gave her a measuring look and then seemed to make up her mind. 'Judy,' she said. 'I know you won't like my saying this, but I think you should tell him about Robin.'

'I know what you think,' said Judy bitterly. She rose from the table and walked across to the window. Laying her head against the cool glass, she stared out at the red and green lights of a fishing boat, sailing slowly away from the shelter of the port towards the darkness of the open sea.

'He has a right to know,' Kate persisted.

'That's what you said when I first found out I was pregnant,' said Judy irritably. 'But have you forgotten the circumstances? All right, I admit that I'd been in love with him for years, but he scarcely even knew I existed, and you know it, Kate. He just fell into bed with me one night after a party when we'd both had too much to drink. By the time I realised what had happened, he'd left the country and he was engaged to somebody else. How could I possibly tell him?'

'You should have trusted him enough for that,' persisted Kate. 'It's not just something trivial, you know. A baby is important.'

'You don't have to tell me that,' retorted Judy. Her lips tightened with the effort to hold back more tears.

'Oh, I'm sorry,' said Kate warmly. 'I know how much you've been through to keep Robin, and you've done a terrific job. Nobody could have done better. It's just that —'

'Kate—' began Judy warningly.

They were interrupted by a joyful yelp, as Robin flung open the living-room door and came hurtling in, followed by Kate's daughter Tamsin. Robin skidded to a halt, then flung himself on his mother. Judy buried her face in his glossy dark hair and held him close.

'Well, what did you do today?' she asked. 'Did you go for a walk with Aunty Kate?'

'No, silly We went to playgroup. Thursdays are always playgroup days, aren't they, Aunty Kate? And I made you a paper mouse, Mummy. It's a very good mouse, but stupid Tamsin tore it.' He wriggled down from Judy's lap and scrabbled in a satchel on the floor. 'Here you are,' he said proudly.

Judy took the tattered cardboard mouse gravely and held it up to admire it. Its pink back had been ripped and mended liberally with sticky tape, and its ears were crooked.

'It's beautiful,' she said. 'But I hope you didn't hurt Tamsin when she tore it.'

'No,' said Robin. 'I just pushed her over in the Play-doh. Judy winced. 'I can see you're going to have a way with women when you're grown up,' she said. 'Well, come on. Get your bag and your parka and say goodbye to Aunty Kate. It's time I started making dinner.'

'Goodbye, Aunty Kate.'

'Goodbye, sweetheart. And don't look so upset, Judy. I have a feeling it'll all work out somehow.'

'Yes, sure,' said Judy listlessly. She picked up her bag. 'Come down for a drink later, if you feel like it, Kate.'

'All right,' lied Kate, looking anxiously at Judy's drawn face. 'And cheer up, won't you?'

It was eight-thirty by the time Judy had wrestled Robin into bed, washed the dinner dishes and vacuumed the flat. With a sigh, she put a tape in the cassette player, switched on the corner lamp and kicked off her shoes. Then she poured herself a large glass of ginger ale, settled back on the sofa and closed her eyes.

The music swept over her in a haunting wave. She had chosen the tape at random, and it was a bad choice for tonight.

A wistful folk song that had been popular nearly five years ago. Alex had liked it too, she knew that. He had played it one night at the folk club on his guitar, while she sat unnoticed in the shadows, gazing at him. Now her lips moved soundlessly with the words.

'Let him only some day, one day, touch my hair again.'

'Oh, damn it!' she cried, leaping to her feet and switching off the tape. She fumbled in the drawer, found a Rachmaninov tape and turned that on instead. Then she took a large gulp of her drink and walked across the room.

'This is ridiculous, Mr Ossi,' she said shakily, stopping in the corner, where a large, articulated skeleton on a wire stand hung grinning cadaverously in the lamplight. 'I have to get a grip on myself. Kate will be here soon.'

As if in answer to her thoughts, there was a ring at the door. Judy gave an impish giggle, looked around her, and then snatched a long-stemmed red rose from a vase on the mantelpiece and thrust it between Mr Ossi's teeth. She stood back briefly to admire her handiwork. Dressing up Mr Ossi had become quite a game for her and Kate, and at various times he had been decorated with a pipe and knitted cap, a bushwalker's balaclava, a large bunch of grapes, and a string of Italian sausages clenched firmly between his strong white teeth.

'Anyone care to tango?' cried Judy, hurrying to the front door and flinging it open. Her heart almost stopped as she saw who was standing there. 'Oh, my goodness,' she whispered.

'Aren't you going to invite me in?' said Alex Shaw, with a wry smile.

'No,' said Judy faintly. 'No, you can't. . . I . . .'

'Judy,' said Alex firmly, 'I know about it all. Kate phoned me about an hour ago and told me. I want to see my son and I want to talk to you, so that's all there is to it.'

Before she knew it, he was inside the tiny hall, hanging up his coat as if he owned the place. Part of her mind registered that it was a very nice coat—a Burberry, elegantly cut and obviously expensive. Completely out of place next to her old duffel coat and Robin's shabby parka. The rest of her brain refused to believe that this was actually happening. Alex came to her rescue and took the glass from her nerveless fingers. He sniffed enquiringly at it.

'Ginger ale?' he asked with a lift of the eyebrows. 'You weren't a ginger-ale girl back in the days when I used to know you.'

'That was in the days when I was young and stupid,' Judy retorted.

'As opposed to now, when you're middle-aged and sensible,' said Alex. 'Well, that should make this all a little easier. Look, Judy, you've had a shock. I suppose I should give you hot tea with sugar, but just this once I think we'll settle for something a little stronger. How about a brandy?'

'I suppose you think I keep brandy in my drinks cabinet all the time on the off-chance that you might drop in, do you?' demanded Judy sarcastically.

'No, I don't, you little spitfire,' said Alex, producing a bottle-shaped paper bag from under his arm. 'I came prepared. So just sit down like a good girl, have a drink and listen to what I have to say.'

To her surprise and annoyance, Judy found herself propelled back into the living-room and settled on the sofa. Alex moved around calmly as if he owned the place, finding glasses and a soda siphon. A low chuckle escaped him as he caught sight of Mr Ossi in the corner, then he fell silent and walked slowly round the room like an insurance assessor. Judy felt sure that nothing was escaping his attention, from the water-marks on one wall, camouflaged by a couple of Robin's paintings, to the worn vinyl on the kitchen floor, just visible through the archway. Yet, for all her irritation, she could not help admiring his pantherlike grace. He was taller than average, with brooding dark eyes and a powerful body. Even the well-cut Italian sports shirt and trousers could not disguise the strength of those hard muscles. Seeing him in such a tiny living-room was like watching a wild animal pacing round a cage.

'Here you are,' he said. 'Now, drink up, and then we'll talk. Cheers!'

'You must be joking,' said Judy, staring incredulously at the hefty tot of brandy in her glass. 'I'll be tiddly for a month on this.'

'All the better for what I have in mind, said Alex cryptically. 'Now, come on. Swallow.'

Obediently Judy took a gulp from the glass. She choked as the fiery liquid ran down her throat. Her limbs felt as if they were turned to water.

'You shouldn't have come here,' she said weakly.

'Yes, I should,' said Alex firmly. 'And I'd have been here nearly five years ago if I'd known what I know now. Why didn't you tell me, Judith?'

His eyes were dark and searching, so like Robin's that it was unnerving. She took another hasty swallow of her drink.

'I —you see—oh, how can I possibly explain? It was all just a terrible mistake. I knew you didn't really care about me, and by the time I realised I was pregnant you'd already left for Canada. And you were engaged to Stephanie Hargreaves. What was I supposed to do? Send you an aerogramme on your honeymoon, saying, "Hi. Remember me? I'm Judy What's-Her-Name, the third-year med student you went to bed with once after a party. Oh, and by the way, I'm pregnant."'? I just couldn't do it.'

'Well, you should have,' said Alex curtly, looking into his glass. 'Anyway, there wasn't any honeymoon.'

'Oh,' said Judy dully. 'Were you too busy to go away?'

'No,' said Alex and a spasm passed across his face. 'There wasn't any honeymoon, because there wasn't any wedding. Stephanie ditched me.'

'I'm sorry,' said Judy impulsively, putting her hand out and touching his. But for some inexplicable reason a dizzy, bubbling feeling started up inside her, as if she had been drinking champagne instead of brandy.

Alex gave her a startled glance, then his warm fingers covered hers. There was a painful, faraway look in his eyes, and he heaved a sigh, but said nothing.

'I—I hope it wasn't because of us,' said Judy timidly.

Alex gave a harsh laugh and released her hand.

'Because of us?' he said, putting down his glass and rising to his feet. 'No. It wasn't "because of us". That didn't mean a thing, as you well know.'

Judy felt a stab of pain pass through her as he said this, and she bit her lip, but Alex scarcely seemed to notice. He walked restlessly across to the window and twitched aside the curtain, so that he could gaze out at the dark vista of the river. Then he continued to talk, with his back turned to her.

'It was just one of those things you do when you're young and stupid,' he said heavily. 'And it would never have happened if I hadn't been so fed up with Stephanie always chasing anything in trousers. I wanted to pay her back, show her what it felt like, but she couldn't have cared less. The funny thing was that I still wanted her so badly, no matter what she did. I couldn't blame other men for lusting after her, either. The minute she walked into a room, every red-blooded male in it was after her as if she were a bitch on heat. I suppose it was that gorgeous figure she had, with the legs that seemed to go on forever. Or maybe it was her silvery blonde hair, or those amazing violet eyes.'

'Probably,' agreed Judy drily.

'Anyway,' said Alex, as if he had not even heard the interruption, 'I couldn't believe it when she accepted my proposal, but I should have known it wouldn't work out. I'd only been in Canada a fortnight when I got a "Dear John" letter from her, saying that she was marrying somebody else. Some irresistible Mr Moneybags with a BMW and a Swiss bank account. I just wasn't in the race.'

'That's a pity,' said Judy. She wondered if he would notice the irony in her voice.

'Well, so how about you?' asked Alex, turning back from the window. 'What have you been doing since I saw you last?'

'Med school,' replied Judy curtly. 'My baby.'

Alex's face was suddenly lit by compassion and interest. 'You must have had a hard time,' he said sympathetically.

'You could say that.'

'Did you take a year off to have the baby?'

'No,' said Judy. 'I took a weekend off to have the baby.'

'A weekend?' asked Alex in an appalled voice.

'I couldn't afford any more!' snapped Judy. 'Either the time or the money. My parents had to scrimp and save for years to send me to med school, as it was. And I might have lost my place in the quota too. You know how much competition there is for places in the clinical school. Besides, I wasn't brilliant like you. Just good average, that's all I ever was. And persistent with it. Anyway, Robin hasn't really suffered from it. He's doing fine.'

'I suppose so,' said Alex dubiously. 'But how on earth did you manage? Who looked after him while you were training at the hospital?'

'Kate did, most of the time,' said Judy. 'I really couldn't have done it all without her. You see, we've been best friends for years, and her marriage broke up just about the time Robin was born, so she offered me this flat at her place. Oh, I pay rent, but nothing like what the place is really worth. She has a little girl, Tamsin, who's six months older than Robin, and they get on really well together. Kate used to mind them both full time, but now she's working three days a week in the clinical library so they go to the crèche sometimes. But you needn't worry about Robin. I take good care of him.'

'I'm sure you do,' said Alex. 'And there's no need to be so defensive. I just wish I'd known so that I could have helped you. But that's all over now. It's the present that counts, and I'd like to see him.'

'He's asleep,' said Judy evasively.

For years she had dreamt of Alex coming in like this, sitting here in the firelit glow of her living-room, banishing her loneliness. But now that it had actually happened, she felt not so much elated as frightened. Scarcely aware of what she was doing, she moved to the door and blocked his way.

'You look like a cornered kitten, standing there with your fur up and your claws ready,' teased Alex. And he leant forward and ruffled her hair with his fingers.

'Stop it!' said Judy, tears starting to her eyes.

'Look, what are you frightened of, Judy? He's my son. I want to see him. It's only natural.'

'You'll just upset him,' she cried. 'It's only a sort of peepshow to you, but he's my whole life, he's everything I've got. Don't you understand? I don't want you coming in here, telling him you're his father, getting him all excited because he thinks he's finally got a daddy like the other kids at playgroup, and then disappearing off to the other side of the world again. It's just not fair. And, besides, you'll wake him up.'

Alex took hold of her shoulders. She felt his hands, warm and comforting through her thin shirt, and the tears spilled out of her eyes and rolled down her cheeks.

'Judy, don't cry. Look at me, damn you! That's better. Now

listen. I'm not going to do any of what you said, and I promise I won't ever tell him I'm his father until I have your permission to do so. OK? I won't even wake him up. But I do want to see him. So are you going to take me to his room, or am I going to pick you up and take you there?'

With a slight shudder, Judy gave in. She took the handkerchief Alex was holding out, mopped her face and then gave him a watery smile. 'All right,' she murmured. 'But did anyone ever tell you you're a bully?'

'Lots of people,' he agreed cheerfully, stuffing the sodden handkerchief back into his pocket. 'It's just part of my fatal charm. Now, come and show me Robin.'

Nothing could have prepared Judy for the emotion she felt on seeing Alex's first glimpse of his son. The bedroom was lit by the warm rosy glow of a night-light, and Robin had fallen asleep on his back with one arm flung up on his pillow. Alex knelt beside the bed and gazed longingly at the sleeping child, overcome by the depth of his own feelings. He looked at the ruffled dark hair, so like his own, the smooth olive skin, and the silky eyelashes that lay like tiny feathers on the boy's cheeks. Then he glanced swiftly round the bedroom, his gaze taking in the colourful murals of elephants and giraffes, the display of blobby playgroup paintings and the worn pair of little slippers next to the bed. Four lost years, he mused, thinking with an ache of nostalgia of all he had missed. For a moment he did not trust himself to speak, then he rose to his feet.

'Come into the living-room,' he whispered to Judy. 'There's something I have to say to you.'

She followed him reluctantly, tears still prickling at the back of her eyes, too enmeshed in her own thoughts to care what Alex had to say. That moment in Robin's room would remain etched in her memory forever, a bitter picture of what she was never going to have. A real family. Father, mother and child together at last. Except that in a minute Alex was going to put on his coat and disappear out of her life, leaving her lonelier than ever.

'Judy?'

'I'm sorry. Did you say something?'

'Yes, I did,' he said impatiently. 'And it's important, so please stop mooning around and listen. I want to ask you something.'

'Go on, then,' she said without interest.

'Will you marry me?'

It was a moment before the full shock sank in. When it did, Judy slid down on to the sofa and took a hasty gulp of brandy. It went down so fast that it made her throat burn and her eyes water.

'What did you say?' she asked in an incredulous voice.

Alex grinned and sat down beside her. 'I asked you if you'd marry me,' he said.

'You must be joking.'

'Come now, Dr Lacey. That's hardly flattering. And, as it happens, I'm completely serious.'

'You really want to marry me?' asked Judy.

'Yes.'

'But why?'

'Isn't it obvious?' asked Alex.

'Not to me,' said Judy in bewilderment.

Alex reached out and took her hand. For a moment she seemed ready to pull it away, then she left it there, fluttering like a frightened bird under his fingers.

'Look,' he said. 'I won't pretend I'm madly in love with you or anything like that, but, as I see it, there are advantages to both of us in getting married.'

A thrill of sadness went through Judy at his easy dismissal of love, but she tried to match his casual tone. 'Such as?' she asked jauntily.

'Well, in the first place there's Robin. He needs a father and I want to be with him. Maybe I wouldn't have wound up with you if things had been different, but I'm thirty-two years old and I'm ready to settle down. You've already had my son, so marrying you seems like the obvious thing to do. I can see from this place that you know how to run a house, and Kate says you're a great cook. And even if you're not ravishingly beautiful, you're quite pretty. You'll do me, anyway.'

'Thank you,' said Judy in a dangerous voice. 'How kind of you, lord and master. So, if I understand you correctly, what you get out of this little marriage of convenience is unlimited access to your son, free housekeeping, meals on the table, and the sexual gratification of a wife who is just about pretty enough to measure up to your exacting standards. And what exactly do I get? Piles of dirty dishes, the privilege of ironing your shirts, and free plastic surgery if my looks turn out not to be quite up to par?'

'Come on, Judy,' pleaded Alex. 'Don't be like that! That wasn't what I meant at all. It just came out the wrong way.'

'I know exactly what you meant!' said Judy angrily. 'And I've never felt so humiliated in my life. You can take your stupid proposal and get out of my flat. So there!'

With a sob of outrage, she leapt to her feet and flung the contents of her brandy glass into his face.

'You little wildcat!' raged Alex.

Before she knew what had happened, Judy felt his fingers biting into her arms like pincers. He was so close that she could see his wildly dilated pupils and feel the frantic thudding of his heart. He stared angrily into her eyes, then suddenly his mouth came down over hers in a savage, passionate kiss. She tasted the brandy on his lips, and for a moment she struggled furiously, twisting and turning in his grasp. Then he shifted his grip, putting his arms around her back and drawing her more closely into his embrace. Angrily she lashed out with her foot, and had the satisfaction of feeling him wince as she struck his shin, but he only kissed her harder. His mouth came down on hers, forcing her lips apart. She closed her eyes for a moment, as if she were drowning, and then the fight went right out of her. Languorously she felt the sweetness of his tongue against hers, and she sighed and nestled closer against his chest, lifting her mouth to his. Glancing up for a moment, she saw the surprise in his face, followed by a mounting excitement. His fingers were sending delicious tremors through her spine, but now they came up and played lazily with her silky hair. His lips moved away from hers and travelled gently across her cheek, before alighting like twin butterflies on her neck. She felt the warm stirring of his breath against her ear and a low moan escaped her.

When he drew her down on to the couch, it seemed the most natural thing in the world for his fingers to move down her body, moulding and caressing it as if it were melted wax. His touch was so light and skilful that she scarcely felt him unbuttoning her blouse. Then suddenly the confining material was gone and her breasts were tingling under his lips. She stretched luxuriously, arching her back and surrendering to the pleasure of his mouth on her naked flesh. He gave a sudden gasp, and then he was on his feet, flinging away his own clothes in wild haste. A moment later his full weight came down on top of her, hard and lusty and male. She felt his muscles like whipcords, the urgent pressure of his lips on hers, the frantic thudding of his heart. Then she surrendered herself completely to him, her body moving in rhythm with his, her soft flesh yielding beneath him, until the most exquisite pleasure flooded through her and she cried out with joy.

Later, much later, as they were lying together in the cramped intimacy of the sofa, Alex raised himself on his elbow and looked down into the blissful sleepiness of her face.

'Judy?'

'Mmm?' She opened her eyes and smiled at him, a shy, fleeting smile that sent dimples chasing around the corners of her mouth.

'Say you'll marry me.'

The dimples vanished. Her eyes grew suddenly troubled.

'I don't know, Alex,' she said hesitantly. 'I need time to think.'

CHAPTER TWO

'WHAT do you mean—you need time to think? What is there to think about?' asked Kate incredulously.

Judy shrugged her shoulders helplessly. 'Everything,' she said. She gazed down the long, rolling green lawn of the park to the wooden pirate ship where Tamsin and Robin were gaily walking the plank against the stunning blue backdrop of the river. Robin tumbled to his knees in the sand and bounced up again, shouting with laughter. Judy's eyes softened as she watched him clambering back up the rigging. My son, she thought. Alex's son. A shiver passed through her.

'Honestly, Kate, I could murder you for landing me in all this,' she said with feeling. 'How could you? I must have lost ten years off my life when Alex showed up last night, and, as if that weren't bad enough, he's picking me up from work tonight. He says he wants to meet Robin properly. Oh, and after that, just to round off the evening, he's taking me out to dinner so that I can give him an answer to his proposal. I told him I needed time to think, so that's what I'm getting. Twenty-four hours. And, in case you're wondering, you're babysitting. That's his lordship's pronouncement, too.'

Kate gave an unrepentant chuckle. 'I'll be glad to,' she said. 'I like a man who's decisive about what he wants. Oh, and, if you want my opinion ——'

'I don't!' interjected Judy.

'—you should say yes to his proposal,' finished Kate calmly. 'After all, you've been in love with him for years. So why don't you be like the kids down there? Just close your eyes and jump.'

'Is that what you did?' asked Judy sharply.

'Ouch!' said Kate. 'All right, I freely admit it. My marriage didn't work out. But I was only nineteen and I didn't even know which way was up. And Doug wasn't much better. Besides, we never had any money, and when Tamsin arrived it just seemed as if we were completely trapped. It'll be different for you and Alex. He's got everything sorted out already. He's travelled all over the world, he's making a fortune, he knows what he wants. And look at you. You're twenty-five years old, you're a qualified doctor, you've already got your life together.'

'I thought I had,' said Judy doubtfully.

'Then what's bothering you?' asked Kate.

Judy looked down for a moment before answering. Nervously, she pleated the edge of her skirt between her fingers. 'He doesn't love me,' she said huskily.

'Oh, love,' said Kate in a wry voice. She stared out at the river, where a schooner was heeled over, beating to windward, fighting for every inch of the way as it came upstream.

'Don't say "love" like that, as if it were a dirty word,' said Judy. 'It matters.'

Kate heaved a sigh. 'I know it does,' she admitted. 'But not as much as you think, and probably not the way you think. And, anyway, you love him, you've already admitted you do. So isn't that enough?'

'No!' cried Judy. 'Oh, don't you see, Kate? That just makes it worse. If I didn't love him, I could probably cope with some horrible marriage of convenience. But, as it is, I couldn't bear it if I thought he was only staying with me because of Robin. And I'd just hate it if he were involved with other women. I'd rather stay unmarried any day.'

'Is that what he wants?' asked Kate. 'Just a marriage of convenience, with other women on the side?'

'I don't know!' exclaimed Judy irritably. 'I don't know what he wants.'

'Then don't you think you should find out?' asked Kate calmly. 'Look, Jude, it's no use getting yourself worked up into a panic about this. Just go out to dinner with him tonight and ask him what his intentions are. Get him to produce the Thirty-Nine Articles of the marriage contract, or whatever it is that he has in mind. And, if it doesn't suit you, say no. At least you'll get a good dinner out of it. Where's he taking you, anyway?'

'The Aragosta.'

'Oooh! Some people have all the luck. Have you got anything to wear?'

'Yes. No. I don't know. I don't care! If I don't get to work in five minutes, Professor Castle is going to hang, draw and quarter me. Look, I'll see you about five-thirty when we come for Robin. OK?'

'OK.'

It was twenty to nine when Judy arrived at work. The first time I've ever been late, she thought irritably, except when Robin had croup last year. And it's all Alex's fault. She found a vicious kind of satisfaction in her rage at him. As she stitched and bandaged and took admission details throughout the morning, she held a series of imaginary dialogues with him in which she told him with great verve and wit how arrogant, overbearing and conceited he was. But, even here, her unruly imagination ran riot, and she found herself dreaming of a scene with Alex which involved far more fiery caresses than humble apologies.

She had half hoped that he might pop into Casualty to see her, but the morning dragged by with no sign of him, and shortly after lunch there was suddenly a red alert as the victims of a three-car road accident were rushed in. Judy found herself so busy and frantic that she had little time to think of anything but emergency action. But late in the afternoon the chance she had been hoping for finally came, and she was sent up to Paediatrics to set up an IV line for a child with gastro-enteritis.

A quick glance soon confirmed that Alex was nowhere in sight, and Judy felt a pang of unreasonable disappointment. You idiot, she told herself bracingly. Stop thinking about Alex! There's work to be done here. The nurse was already standing by with the equipment neatly laid out, and Judy ran her eyes over the cannula and the giving set and nodded approvingly. Then she gave an injection of lignocaine as a local anaesthetic in the little girl's arm, and, as soon as it had gone to work, put a tourniquet on the arm, got the vein up and put the needle in. But all the time she was working she kept half expecting that Alex would suddenly materialise beside her.

When she had finished setting up the drip, she glanced at her watch and saw that it was after five-thirty. A slight pang of disappointment went through her. No chance of seeing Alex now, she thought wistfully, but at least she could call in and make a quick visit to Michael Burrows before she went home. She strode swiftly down the corridor and stopped at the sister's office to ask which ward he was in.

'Michael Burrows?' said the sister, doing a double-take. 'Oh, no! What's he up to now?'

'Nothing, as far as I know,' said Judy in a puzzled voice. 'I admitted him yesterday and I just want to pop in and see him. Why? Has he been giving you trouble?'

'Trouble isn't the word for it!' replied the sister with feeling. 'He got right out of the ward this morning, and I never even saw him go. We finally found him two floors down with one of the other kids, giving each other rides on a trolley. If he's like this when he's sick, he must be an awful handful when he's well!'

Judy winced sympathetically. 'Which bed is he in?' she asked, peering down the ward.

'The one at the end. And don't let the drawn curtains fool you. I just closed them because he was shooting paper pellets at the other kids with a catapult.'

As Judy came closer to the curtained cubicle, she heard a rapid 'Pow! Pow! Pow!' followed by a low cry of triumph. She stifled a grin and twitched back the curtain.

'May I come in?' she asked.

Michael was sitting up in bed, hunched over a hand-held electronic game. He looked up eagerly, but some of the eagerness went out of his face when he saw Judy. Nevertheless, he managed a smile.

'Hello, Dr Lacey,' he said politely. 'I thought you were my mum. Did you see her on the way in?'

'Sorry, Michael,' said Judy, shaking her head. 'Did you manage to wipe out all the aliens?'

His smile revived. Generously he offered her a turn with the game, and for a few minutes there was no sound apart from Michael's excited chatter and the noisy destruction of the universe. Then, just as Judy was about to get up and leave, the curtain twitched open again. Michael's face brightened for a moment, and then fell as a tall, thin, stern-faced man with greying hair came in. He was dressed in a neat, dark business suit and looked like a lawyer or accountant.

'You must be Dr Lacey,' he said, stretching out his hand. 'How do you do? I'm Adrian Burrows, Michael's father.'

Michael opened his mouth as if about to protest, and then said nothing. He put down the game and settled back into his pillows, looking suddenly very pale and miserable.

'What happened to Mum?' he whispered.

'She had to stay late at work to make up the time she missed yesterday bringing you in. But she'll come and see you after dinner. I brought you some books.'

Michael turned his head away. 'Thanks,' he said dully.

Judy made her excuses and left. It was nearly six o'clock

and she had a child of her own to think about, but she could not help puzzling over the scene she had just witnessed. Something was obviously troubling Michael, and that fact niggled at Judy as she made her way out of the building. Michael had a major operation in front of him and his mental state was important. It might be something quite silly and trivial that was bothering him—children often worked themselves into a state over the most extraordinary things—but Judy felt that he needed help. She decided to mention it to Alex when he came to collect her. If he did. With any luck he had probably decided by now that the whole thing was sheer lunacy and gone back to Canada. Well, good, thought Judy, coming out a side door and looking around the car park with an exasperated sigh. It is lunacy!

'Bad day?' asked a sympathetic voice.

It was Alex. He fell into step beside her and took her arm. Her first impulse was to snatch it away, but then his grip felt so firm and comforting that she left it there. She heaved a deep sigh and nodded.

'Yes,' she said. 'No. I mean no. It was frantically busy this afternoon. There was a three-car crash out on the Brooker Highway and it was touch and go whether a couple of them would make it, but I think they're all going to survive. I suppose that's a good day.'

'The best,' he agreed companionably. 'But how was your morning?'

She made a face.

'Old ladies' bunions,' she said. 'Unspeakable instant coffee. Prof Castle ready to have my guts for garters because I was ten minutes late arriving at work.'

Alex clicked his tongue reprovingly. 'That'll teach you to stay up all night with dissipated young men,' he growled in a fair imitation of Professor Castle's voice. 'And it's to be hoped, Dr Lacey, that you don't make a habit of this sort of thing.'

'I don't!' replied Judy coldly. 'And he wasn't a dissipated young man.'

'Ah, well,' said Alex, grinning. 'Not dissipated, eh?'

'No,' said Judy. 'Not young. I'd call him middle-aged.'

'You cheeky little twerp!' exclaimed Alex. 'I've a good mind to make you walk home for that. But, seeing you look so grotty and exhausted, I'll take pity on you just this once. Now, hop in here.'

Judy swung round to find that he was patiently holding open the door of an immaculate navy-blue Mercedes Benz. Its paintwork was so highly polished that she could see her pale face and old coat reflected back at her, and the interior was beyond description. Plush and opulent with a faint, expensive scent of spicy cologne, it positively gleamed with chrome and velvet and shiny gadgets. Judy gulped.

'Nice, isn't it?' said Alex casually, climbing into the driver's seat. 'My father gave it to me for my birthday last year.'

'Oh,' replied Judy. 'My dad gave me a car for my birthday once too. It was a 1967 Mini with a dent in the left fender and a hole in the back seat where his kelpie had chewed the upholstery. It went quite well, though. Sometimes.'

'What happened to it?' asked Alex.

'I've still got it, but it's being repaired. The gear stick came off in my hand last week.'

'Never mind,' said Alex, reaching out and deftly twiddling a knob. The gay tones of a Renaissance harpsichord sprang into the air. 'I'll buy you a new car when we're married.' There was a frosty silence as he reversed out of the parking space. 'I said I'll buy you a new car when we're married,' said Alex in a dangerous voice.

'I heard you,' said Judy sourly.

'Thank you, Alex,' said Alex gratefully. 'That'll be lovely. It'll be nice not to have to drive around in a clapped-out old wreck, risking my life and my child's. How thoughtful of you!'

'Oh, go to hell!' retorted Judy, staring angrily at the street ahead of them.

'Are you always so prickly?' demanded Alex.

'Only when men offer to buy me cars,' retorted Judy.

'Oh, a thousand pardons, ma'am. I just thought it would be rather nice for my wife and son to drive around in a decent vehicle that would give them a bit of comfort and safety. I had no idea I was offering you a mortal insult.'

'I'm not your wife!' cried Judy, stung by his sarcasm.

'Not yet,' agreed Alex complacently. 'But you will be.'

'You are insufferable!' raged Judy. 'You sleek, self-satisfied, overpaid, overbearing, fatuous oaf! Do you think you only have to snap your fingers and I'll come running?'

'Yes!' agreed Alex mildly. 'And you forgot handsome.'

'Handsome?' demanded Judy.

'Yes. Sleek, self-satisfied, overpaid . . . what was it? Overpaid? Overbearing? But irresistibly handsome.'

Judy cast him a smouldering look and then burst out laughing. 'Oh, you're impossible!' she cried. 'Do you always get what you want?'

'Usually,' said Alex calmly.

'Except for Stephanie Hargreaves?' demanded Judy with a touch of malice.

At once she could have bitten out her tongue. The laughter died out of Alex's eyes and a cold, brooding look came into his face. 'Everyone's entitled to one failure.' he said sombrely.

He did not speak again until they rounded the curve of Princes Wharf and came into Salamanca Place. The old sandstone warehouses were floodlit with soft yellow light, and the oak trees in front of Parliament House wore a mist of new spring leaves. If it had not been for the huge cargo ships with their superstructures towering white and gleaming against the darkening sky, they might have been travelling back in time to the old colonial days. Alex pulled the car off a bend in the road just past the CSIRO marine laboratories. In spite of herself, Judy felt her heartbeat quicken. It was a place where lovers often parked—with a long, sweeping view of the dark blue river already bathed in the shimmering glow of the full moon. As Alex switched off the purring engine, Judy heard the mournful cry of plovers overhead, and felt the blood pulsing swiftly through her veins. But Alex's voice was disappointingly matter-of-fact.

'I've bought something for Robin,' he said. 'But I thought I'd better check with you first, in case you think it's unsuitable.'

He groped into the darkness of the seat behind him and lifted the lid off a bulky carton. Then he reached for the overhead light. For a moment Judy's eyes were dazzled by the sudden brightness, then she saw what was in the box.

'What's the matter?' asked Alex anxiously. 'Don't you like it? Or do you think it's too big for him? The saleswoman said it was a very safe model. I wouldn't have bought it otherwise.'

'It's not that,' said Judy. She reached out to touch the pedal car, unable to believe her eyes. This was no plastic toyshop rubbish that would fall apart on the second day. It was made of solid metal, its joints beautifully welded, its red paintwork as shiny as that of Alex's Mercedes. Attached to its windshield was a gold klaxon, which let out a blaring protest under Alex's long fingers, and on the leather seat was a nifty little safety helmet with matching goggles.

'Well, what do you think?' asked Alex.

'It's—it's beautiful,' said Judy in bewilderment. 'But where on earth did you get it? I've never seen anything like this in Hobart.'

'No, well, actually I bought it in Melbourne,' said Alex. 'I was there this morning.'

'In Melbourne?' demanded Judy in an incredulous voice. 'You flew all the way to Melbourne just to buy a toy car for Robin?'

'Well, not only for that,' said Alex. 'I had to go over anyway, on business. My father's firm is based there, and I'm one of the directors. But there's something wrong, isn't there? Don't you like it?'

Judy bit her lip, trying to sort out her own confusion. A warm feeling swept over her as she imagined Alex amid all the hurly burly of airports and directors' meetings, slipping out to buy a car for Robin. Her own little Robin, whose toys so far had been mostly well-chewed hand-me-downs from other children, or home-made contrivances of glue and plywood. The warm feeling was succeeded by a sharp pang of jealousy. Then she struggled to be fair.

'I don't want to be down on everything you do, Alex,' she said. 'I think the pedal car's great and Robin will love it, but it does bother me a bit. I guess it's partly just that I'm jealous. I could never afford to give him anything like that, and I feel I simply can't compete——'

'It's not a competition——' Alex began, but she silenced him with a swift look from her clear green eyes.

'— but it's not only that,' she finished. 'Look, I do want Robin to get to know you, whatever happens. But I want him to build a relationship with you because of what you are, not because of what you give him. Does that make sense?'

Alex winced and sat back in his seat. He heaved a deep sigh. 'Yes,' he said at last. 'Perfect sense. And you're quite right, Judy. Consciously or not, I probably was hoping to buy him. Look, when's his birthday?'

'September the twenty-sixth. Why?'

'Well, that's only a week or two from now. Why don't we put the car away until then, and you can give it to him for a birthday present?' he suggested.

Disbelief and excitement fled across her face. 'Oh, Alex! Could I?' she cried.

His arms came out and drew her to him. Then he kissed her affectionately on the forehead. 'Oh, Judy,' he said teasingly. 'If you could only see yourself! You look like a kid who's just had a visit from Santa. Well, come on. Now that I've demonstrated the purity of my motives, how about letting me meet Robin?'

The porch light was already on when they reached home, and a muted but distant uproar seemed to be going on in the back of the house. When Judy rang Kate's doorbell, the uproar came closer. A flustered Kate with a splash of chocolate pudding mix on her cheek opened the door with one hand, while the other hand kept a firm hold on a writhing, bellowing child.

'Hi, Judy. Hello, Alex,' she said hastily. 'Look, I'm sorry about this, but Robin wouldn't take a nap this afternoon, and he's being absolutely poisonous.'

A long, thunderous roar confirmed this. Judy crouched down on her knees and put out her arms to the wildly hiccuping child.

'Robin,' she said calmly, 'what's the matter?'

More roars. An outburst of foot-stamping, followed by some hysterical mumbling. Then Robin buried his face in her shoulder and great earthquake sobs shook his tiny frame.

'I can't understand a word you're saying, sweetheart,' said Judy.

He lifted his swollen, tear-stained face to hers and began to gulp out his grievances. In that moment Alex stood as if riveted to the spot. It was uncanny, the resemblance the child bore to him. The raven-dark hair, the smouldering brown eyes, even the arrogant lift to the chin were immediately recognisable. And so was the temper. A pang of sympathy for Judy went through him, as he watched her smoothing the little boy's hair, kissing away his tears. He remembered what a rotten time he had given his own mother, but she at least had had a husband and other children to share the strain. How did Judy ever cope with this sort of thing alone?

'Is he always like this?' he asked in disbelief.

'Pretty often,' said Judy coldly, still occupied in drying Robin's tears. 'Why? Not quite the image of domestic bliss that you had in mind?'

'Hey, come on,' said Alex, and his hand came down, warm and firm on her shoulder. 'I wasn't being critical, you know.'

Kate glanced anxiously from one of them to the other, and then, with a murmured apology, slipped back into the kitchen.

Judy felt Alex's fingers massaging the tension out of her muscles and unconsciously she sighed with relief. 'That's nice,' she murmured.

'Good,' said Alex, helping her to her feet. 'Well, what's the matter with Robin, then—or shouldn't I ask?'

He put his arm casually around her and led her towards the kitchen, deliberately ignoring the child, but a renewed bout of howling made them both look round. Satisfied that he had gained their attention, Robin stopped crying and held his breath. His face turned red and then purple.

'Robin!' cried Judy, darting back towards him, before Alex's grip on her arm restrained her.

Alex gave a slight shake of his head and then looked down at his hand resting on her sleeve. 'Just look at this, Judy!' he exclaimed. 'It's a Blue Emperor butterfly, isn't it? How on earth did you get that on your coat sleeve? They're pretty rare, aren't they?'

'Yes,' agreed Judy in a choking voice. 'In fact, they're only found in the Amazon jungles, I believe.'

There was a strangled gasp from below as Robin let out his breath. 'Show me!' he demanded, trying to wriggle between the two adults.

As fast as lightning, Alex cupped his hand around the imaginary butterfly. 'Shh!' he ordered. 'You'll have to be very quiet and gentle. They hate noise, Blue Emperors do. They're like your mother. It gives them a headache, so you just tiptoe along to the kitchen, and when you're really nice and quiet I'll bring the butterfly along to you.'

'All right,' whispered Robin, and to Judy's amazement he crept quietly away.

Her eyes, brimming with laughter, met Alex's. 'He'll have a fit when he realises there's no Blue Emperor,' she warned.

'No, he won't,' said Alex confidently. 'Not when I find an Easter egg behind his ear.' And he reached forward and produced a tiny, brightly wrapped chocolate from among Judy's chestnut curls. She let out a gasp of surprise.

'Well, you're a man of many talents!' she exclaimed.

'And you haven't seen half of them yet,' he said in a sultry voice, running a finger teasingly up her spine. 'Now, off you go and have a bath and make yourself beautiful for tonight.'

'I can't!' she protested. 'He's thrown chocolate pudding all over Kate's kitchen floor, the little wretch! I'll have to go and clean it up.'

'Cleaning up chocolate pudding is my greatest talent of all,' said Alex firmly. 'Now, move.'

'But——' began Judy.

'Doctor's orders,' insisted Alex, giving her a gentle shove towards the door. 'You've got a couple of hours before we need to leave. So go and relax for a while.'

Red cars, Blue Emperors, chocolate Easter eggs, thought Judy with a wry smile, as she stumbled down the dark path to her flat and inserted the key in her front door. What next? She soon found out. The moment the light flooded the hall, something green and shimmering caught her eye. With a little cry of amazement she stepped forward to the coat rack and reached out her hand to touch it. The material slipped through her fingers like water, and the tiny silver threads that were woven through it danced and sparkled in the light. She turned it over and examined the label. A designer evening dress, she thought incredulously. Size ten. Alex had even guessed right on that.

On the floor next to her bushwalking boots was a cardboard box with a Melbourne address on it, and when she lifted the lid and drew back the tissue paper she saw that he had thought of everything. Matching silver evening slippers. She did not even bother to check the size on those. She knew they would be perfect. It seemed that everything Alex Shaw owned had to be perfect. A tight, angry expression came over Judy's face and she went into her room to dress for dinner.

'Didn't you like the dress I bought you?' asked Alex.

Judy glanced up from her champagne glass and saw the look of annoyance on his face. A little stab of triumph went through her. He had said nothing when she'd appeared at seven-thirty in the old red dress passed on to her by Kate three years before, and he had been the perfect host all through dinner, but she had been aware of his anger simmering below the surface. To give him credit, he had been more patient than she'd expected. For nearly two hours they had sat eating and chatting, with the firelight flickering over the restaurant walls and the haunting music of a series of Beethoven piano sonatas wafting in from the other room. Delectable scallops, hot and smothered in a mornay sauce with breadcrumbs, had been followed by a juicy tournedos chasseur and the lightest of chocolate mousses, and Alex had maintained his outward calm. But now it seemed the explosion was imminent.

'Well?' he insisted angrily.

Judy licked a final speck of chocolate mousse from her spoon and pushed the bowl away with a sigh of pleasure. A tiny smile hovered around her lips as she dabbed her mouth with the napkin. 'It was wonderful,' she murmured dreamily.

'What was? The dress or the chocolate mousse?'

'Both,' she said.

'Then why didn't you wear it?'

'The dress or the chocolate mousse?' she asked teasingly.

'Judith——' warned Alex. His voice was so sharp that a passing waiter looked round enquiringly and then hurried on.

'People are looking at us,' she hissed furiously.

'Let them,' said Alex indifferently. 'I asked you a question and I want an answer. Why didn't you wear the dress I bought you?'

'Oh, because . . . because it wasn't only a matter of buying the dress, you seem to think you've bought me too. Because you're arrogant and overbearing, and you didn't even ask me if I wanted any new clothes or what I'd like if I did get any. Because I've been supporting myself for years now, and I don't expect you to come in and just take over my life as if I'm some sort of slave.'

Alex leant back in his chair and pressed his fingers together. A look of amusement passed over his face. 'Alex Shaw the White Slave-Trader,' he said reflectively. 'I must say I never really thought of it that way. I just felt there wasn't much time to spare, and you'd probably like a new dress to celebrate our engagement.'

'We're not engaged yet,' said Judy through clenched teeth.

'We soon will be,' Alex continued smoothly. 'But, of course, once we're married I'll give you a Visa card and you can choose your own clothes. Although, judging by what you're wearing tonight, you ought to be grateful for my help. You know, red really doesn't suit you at all. I can't think why you chose it.'

'I didn't choose it,' retorted Judy, unreasonably stung by this criticism. 'Kate did.'

'I see,' said Alex pleasantly. 'So that's why it's two sizes too big for you and makes you look as if you've got yellow fever. You know, you shouldn't grind your teeth like that. It's bad for them.'

'Oh!' exclaimed Judy furiously. 'You're impossible!'

'So I've been told,' said Alex with a sardonic grin. 'But you'll just have to get used to me, won't you?'

'Oh, will I?' demanded Judy.

'Yes,' said Alex softly, but there was a steely undertone in his voice. 'It's one of those things a good wife has to do—adjust to her husband. Two black coffees, please.'

Judy sat in silent outrage while the waiter poured the coffee, but the moment his back was turned her anger burst out. 'What makes you so certain I'm going to be your wife?' she snapped.

Alex stirred his coffee silently for a moment. He was outwardly calm, but there was something about the controlled tension of his movements that made Judy catch her breath. Deliberately he set down his spoon and looked at her. For a moment she held his gaze, then she looked down in confusion. His brown eyes were filled with such implacable hostility that she felt a wild urge to run outside into the sanctuary of the night. Then she felt his fingers, hard and warm and insistent, lifting her chin.

'Look at me, Judith,' he ordered. 'And, for once in your life, just be quiet and listen. You've already robbed me of nearly four years of my son's life, and I don't intend to lose any more of it. You want to know why I'm so certain you're going to be my wife. All right, I'll tell you. Because it's your duty.'

'Duty?' echoed Judy in disbelief.

'Yes, duty,' snapped Alex. 'Go on, laugh, if you want to. I

suppose it seems pretty ridiculous to you. After all, you've probably had a lot of fun being a Women's Libber and bringing up your child on your own.'

'Fun?' demanded Judy in a strained voice.

'In any case,' said Alex, ruthlessly overriding her, 'that's all over now. I'm pretty old-fashioned in a lot of ways, and I happen to believe that it's a lot better for a kid if his parents are married. I won't pretend it's what either of us wants, but I'm certain it's what we should do. As I said before, it's our duty. After all, it's just a practical arrangement for Robin's benefit. Feelings don't come into it.'

'Oh, I see,' said Judy. 'Just a practical arrangement. So I suppose that means we have separate lives and separate beds and separate bank accounts. And, whenever you want to race off with some pretty little nurse or med student, I just look politely the other way. Because, after all, feelings don't come into it. And no doubt you'll be just as accommodating to my little affairs. That sounds like a great marriage to me.'

She rose to her feet, gathering up her bag, her breath coming in ragged gasps. Then Alex's hand closed around her wrist.

'Where do you think you're going?' he demanded.

'Home,' said Judy.

'Oh, no, you're not,' he snapped. 'Now sit down.'

'You're hurting me,' she said through clenched teeth.

'I'll hurt you a lot worse if you don't do as I say.'

Judy glanced around and saw the other diners gazing curiously at them. With a little cry of annoyance she sat down and glared at Alex as he released her. Deliberately she massaged her wrist, her green eyes flashing reproach.

'You've got it all wrong, Dr Lacey,' he said in a voice charged with anger. 'I told you I was old-fashioned. I'm going to marry you, and I won't take no for an answer. But you'd better just get one thing straight. There'll be no separate lives, separate beds or separate bank accounts. The pretty nurses and med students are all in the past, and, if you're ever foolish enough to get involved with another man, I'll personally wring his neck. And yours. Is that clear enough for you?'

'Yes,' whispered Judy.

'All right. Well, stop talking rubbish about love and give me your hand.'

Judy looked frantically round the room. A dessert trolley now stood blocking the way to the exit, and everyone's eyes were on her. There was no escape. In any case, she was no longer sure she wanted to escape. She saw Alex take a small box out of his pocket, glimpsed the flash of emeralds and diamonds. Then, with her heart thudding wildly, she stretched out her hand and watched in disbelief as he slid the engagement ring on to her finger.

CHAPTER THREE

JUDY realised that her engagement to Alex would bring about changes in her life. What she was not prepared for was the speed with which they took place. Or the nervousness she felt about breaking the news to everybody.

Kate, of course, was over the moon when she heard what had happened. As usual when Judy had to stay out late, Robin had stayed the night at Kate's place. When Judy tapped hesitantly at the kitchen door at eight o'clock on Saturday morning, Kate positively dragged her inside.

'Well?' she demanded.

Shyly Judy held out her left hand. Kate let out a whoop of joy and fell on her neck.

'Judy, that's fantastic! Well, I've got to hand it to Alex, he certainly doesn't let the grass grow under his feet. Come and have some coffee and tell me everything!'

'What about the kids?'

'Watching *Play School* on the video,' replied Kate. 'Never mind about them. I want to hear every juicy little detail. This is the most romantic thing that's happened in years!'

'I don't know about romantic,' confessed Judy uneasily. 'You should have heard the things he said to me.'

Haltingly she described the dinner and Alex's proposal in graphic detail. Pride would never have allowed her to be so honest with anyone else, but she and Kate were always brutally frank with each other.

'So you see,' she finished, 'it really isn't romantic at all. Just a businesslike arrangement.'

'Don't worry,' said Kate comfortingly. 'The rest will follow if you just give yourselves time.'

'That's one thing we really don't have,' said Judy ruefully. 'Alex wants the wedding as soon as possible, so we're getting married next month!'

Kate gave a low whistle of astonishment. 'Well, you'd better tell your family and friends right away,' she said, 'before the bush telegraph gets going. An announcement like this is going to be the scoop of the season at St Thomas's.'

'I know,' admitted Judy. 'Alex has already flown off to Melbourne this morning to tell his parents. But I can't say I'm too thrilled about breaking the news to my family. When Dad found out I was pregnant a few years ago, he was ready to hang, draw and quarter the swine who was responsible. It could make things a bit tricky introducing them.'

'I see what you mean!' agreed Kate. 'Still, you'll have to just bite the bullet and get it over with.'

'I suppose so,' sighed Judy. 'But there's just one thing, Kate. All of this is going to be awfully confusing for Robin. I'd like to give him a little more time to get to know Alex before I tell him, so don't say anything to him about it, will you?'

'Trust me,' said Kate.

'And, as for the bunch of private eyes at St Thomas's, they can just find out about it after we're married!'

'Fat chance!' said Kate, rolling her eyes.

When she arrived at work on Monday morning, Judy had to admit that Kate was right. She was barely inside the door when another young intern, Marion Kelly, bounced up to her and embraced her.

'Congratulations on your engagement, Judy!' she cried. 'It's wonderful news!'

Judy's eyes glazed. 'How did you know?' she demanded, looking down at her deliberately ringless finger.

'Oh, Mr Shaw's telling everyone. Hasn't he bought you a

ring yet?'

'Yes,' said Judy indignantly. 'I took it off, because. . . because ——'

'I know. They get in the way in a job like this, don't they? Anyway, I must fly. I'm taking over from you on Casualty this week. By the way, did you know you've been shifted off Geriatrics? You're doing Theatre instead. It's on the notice-board.'

Judy gazed after Marion's retreating figure with a dazed expression. Trust Alex to take the bull by the horns and tell everybody immediately! Oh, well, perhaps it was best to get it over with. And at least she wouldn't have to face the barrage of questions and comments alone. A transfer to Theatre meant that she would probably be working with Alex. Let him deal with the gossip, since he had been so keen to spread the news!

Judy was running through the surgical list over a quick cup of coffee when Alex came into the tea-room at nine-thirty. Nurse Wilcox, who had already heard the incredible news about the couple, pricked up her ears in anticipation as he crossed the room.

'Good morning, Nurse. Good morning, Judy. Any problems with the list?'

Judy glanced up, acutely conscious of the other girl's scrutiny. She felt the blood rush into her cheeks, but to her relief her voice at least remained calm.

'Not really. But I see Michael Burrows is down for exploratory surgery. Has he had tests since I saw him last week?'

Alex flung himself into a chair and smiled warmly at Nurse Wilcox. 'Any chance of a cup of coffee, Nurse?' he wheedled.

She sighed and left the room.

'I didn't really expect to see you today,' said Judy in a carefully neutral voice. 'I thought I'd be starting on Geriatrics this week.'

'I know,' said Alex calmly. 'I had you changed over on the roster.'

'You did what?' demanded Judy in a stunned voice.

'Tim Matthews, who was supposed to be assisting me, has apparently fallen down some stairs and broken a wrist. Somebody had to take his place, so I simply arranged for it to be you. I'll never get a chance to speak to you otherwise, and there are things we need to discuss.'

'Such as?' demanded Judy, feeling unaccountably annoyed by this high-handed behaviour.

'Such as going to Melbourne to visit my parents,' retorted Alex. 'After all, it was a bit of a shock to them to learn that they were about to acquire a new daughter-in-law and grandson. Naturally enough they want to meet you.'

'Oh,' said Judy in a small voice. 'Yes, I suppose so. When do you want to go?'

She could scarcely believe that all this was happening. Details about parents-in-law and trips to Melbourne somehow seemed to make it all true. Frighteningly real and solid.

'This weekend?' suggested Alex.

'I can't. It's Robin's birthday.'

'Next weekend, then.'

'All right,' agreed Judy despairingly. 'But what about Robin? Is he coming too?'

'I'd rather we go alone this time,' said Alex. 'You won't have a chance to get to know them if you're racing around after Robin.'

'I suppose not,' admitted Judy.

'Good, then that's settled,' said Alex with satisfaction, as if they had just solved some minor problem of hospital red tape. 'Now, there are just a few points I want to discuss with you over this Burrows case . . .'

When Nurse Wilcox returned with Alex's coffee, she found the couple immersed in a disappointingly professional discussion.

'So he's had a CAT scan and an intravenous pyelogram?' Judy was asking.

'That's right. And there's a mass suspicious of nephroblastoma in the right abdomen. See he shadow here . . .'

Nurse Wilcox plunked down the coffee, gave another aggrieved sigh and left the room. Out in the dirty-instruments-room, she reported to Staff Nurse Palmer as they scrubbed the Spencer Wells forceps and the Matthieus needle-holders that personally she thought the whole story about the engagement was just a hoax. Anyone listening in to Alex and Judy's conversation would probably have agreed with her.

'So what exactly do you hope to do this morning?' asked Judy.

'I'll open up the abdomen and check the extent of the tumour.' said Alex, frowning down at the pyelogram. 'With luck we'll be able to remove it immediately, but there's a chance it may have spread and attached itself to the aorta or the inferior vena cava. In that case we're in trouble.'

'What will you do if it has?' asked Judy.

'Take a small piece and do a biopsy. But if it's spread as far as I suspect, then his only chance is to go to Melbourne for further surgery with a bigger team.'

'Well, let's hope it doesn't come to that,' said Judy. 'He's such a cute little kid!'

Alex glanced across at her compassionately. 'Rather like Robin to look at,' he agreed. 'Is that what was upsetting you about him last week? The resemblance?'

Judy nodded silently. She was touched that Alex remembered her earlier distress, and she felt a sudden impulse to reach out and touch him. An impulse she sternly suppressed. You're colleagues, she told herself. Working colleagues, just remember that. Staring at his brooding face as he studied the pyelogram, she found it impossible to believe in the events of the previous Friday. Like Nurse Wilcox, she was strongly tempted to believe that the whole engagement was a hoax. Then Alex looked up and smiled. A warm, reassuring smile.

'Don't worry,' he said, reaching out and patting her on the knee. 'Just keep your head and you'll do fine. Remember, you're a lot more use to me if your feelings aren't involved.'

But it took all Judy's self-control to maintain her detachment when the time finally came. Michael's operation was the last of the morning, following an orchidopexy, a hernia and an excision of a mole. Michael had already been given his pre-med and was wheeled into the operating theatre on a trolley. His hair was tucked under a cap and his face wore a vague, drowsy expression. Alex walked over and looked down at the child.

'Hello, Mike,' he said. 'Do you remember me? I'm Mr Shaw. And your old friend Dr Lacey is here too. See her over there?'

Michael gazed around the gowned and masked figures with a puzzled expression.

'Hi, Michael,' said Judy cheerfully.

His face brightened at the familiar voice, and he gave her a cheeky grin, then his eyelids closed, fluttered, opened again.

'Hi, Dr Lacey,' he said in a slurred voice.

'Dr Pryor is going to give you something to put you to sleep,' continued Alex calmly. 'You'll just feel a small prick on the back of your hand, and I want you to count up to ten. OK?'

'OK,' agreed Michael drowsily.

Within a couple of minutes Richard Pryor had the boy completely under and they were all hard at work. Judy had never worked with Alex before, but she was too absorbed to feel nervous. All the time that she was holding the retractors, swabbing away blood, holding the spleen up and pushing the bowel down, a voice kept repeating inside her head, Oh, God, let it be all right. Make it something Alex can deal with.

But it was not all right. Once the tumour was fully exposed, Judy saw that Alex's fears had been only too accurate. The greyish mass not only covered the kidney, but was dangerously entangled with the inferior vena cava. Only major surgery with a large team of experts could possibly save Michael's life. Judy heard her own involuntary gasp of dismay, then Alex's voice rang in her ears, as firm and confident as ever.

'I'm just going to take a piece of this. Get ready to suck away the blood, Dr Lacey.'

After that it was the usual routine of holding retractors, cutting sutures, trying to anticipate Alex's every move, while her heart seemed turned to stone inside her. When Michael was finally wheeled away to the recovery-room, Judy had to blink away the tears before she trusted herself to take off her mask and gown. Even writing up the operation notes was an ordeal. The terse clinical comments seemed so full of poignancy.

'A large tumour was found in the right kidney. It was fifteen centimetres across and it was found to be invading the stomach and inferior vena cava,' she wrote.

She looked down at her small, neat handwriting and gave a tremulous sigh. And what that really means, she thought bitterly, is that this little boy is probably going to die. For one moment of savage misery she wondered why on earth she had ever wanted to be a doctor. Then a warm hand came down on her shoulder.

'Having problems?' asked Alex.

She bit her lip.

'Not really,' she said. 'But I can't help wondering how his mother will take it.'

Alex sat down beside her. 'I've just spoken to her,' he said. 'She took it on the chin—just the way you would.'

Judy gave a wry smile in acknowledgement of this odd compliment, and looked back at her notes. 'So what now?' she asked.

'We'll give him two or three days to let him recover from this operation and then send him to Melbourne. They'll probably order a few tests before they do anything else, but my guess is that they'll operate either on Friday or next Monday. With a bit of luck Michael could be in the clear a week from now.'

Or dead, thought Judy, and a chill went through her. She had no illusions about the danger and difficulty of the operation that faced the little boy. But Alex was right. She could not afford to get involved. Brushing a stray curl back from her forehead, she stood up.

'Well, if there's nothing else to do here, I suppose I should go to lunch,' she said bracingly. 'I've got a pretty heavy afternoon ahead of me.'

She was halfway across the room when Alex caught her up and seized her arm. 'Do you always run out on your fiancés like this?' he asked teasingly. 'I have to eat too, you know. And there are things we need to discuss.'

All the way down in the lift, Judy kept stealing glances at Alex. He was an exceptionally handsome man, but his good looks were of the dark, brooding variety. When he laughed, his face lit up, but in repose it seemed stern and forbidding. He was not laughing now, and his profile looked as cold and severe as if it had been chiselled out of marble. Even in the few short days since he had joined the staff of St Thomas's, he had begun to acquire a reputation. The nurses grumbled that he was a perfectionist, capable of the most blistering sarcasm over any sloppy or unsatisfactory work. Judy wondered with a qualm what sort of husband he would make.

The lift shuddered to a halt and they stepped out into the corridor leading to one of the staff dining-rooms. Almost immediately Alan Randall, a middle-aged osteopath with florid cheeks and a loud voice, came striding towards them and clapped Alex on the shoulder.

'Congratulations!' he boomed. 'I heard the news from Prof Castle. I must say you're a fast worker, Shaw. Only been here a week or two, haven't you?'

Alan's eyes were full of speculation as they moved from Alex down to Judy. She felt her cheeks burning, well aware of the unspoken questions in the air. Did you know she has an illegitimate child? Do you have any idea whose it is? Then Alex's arm came protectively round her shoulder.

'That's right,' he agreed. 'Two weeks, to be exact, but Judy and I go back a lot longer than that, don't we, darling?'

His dark eyes met hers with a warmth that would have melted her heart, if only it had been genuine. But Judy was miserably well aware that he was only doing it to fool the audience. Alex was far too proud to let Alan Randall or anybody else think he was getting married merely out of duty.

'Hrrmph!' said Alan. 'Well, best of luck to both of you!'

And he lumbered away, leaving Judy scarlet with embarrassment. 'I've changed my mind!' she said desperately. 'I'm not coming to the cafeteria. I don't want any lunch.'

'Yes, you do,' said Alex, ruthlessly propelling her into the dining-room.

A trolley full of dirty dishes rumbled past them, forcing them to flatten themselves against the wall.

'Why did you have to tell everyone so quickly?' she

complained. 'I haven't even had time to get used to the idea myself yet!'

Alex smiled, and his face lit up in the way Judy loved. 'If you have something tough to do, it's always better to do it immediately and get it over with,' he said. 'Or, at least, that's been my experience. You must have gone through worse than this when you had Robin, and you survived that. Now, chin up and hold on to me, because we're going to get this over with.'

The next half-hour was a difficult time for Judy. Most of the people who came up to congratulate them were genuinely delighted about the engagement, but a few were curious to the point of rudeness. Judy could not help but admire the skill with which Alex fielded the trickiest questions, and her only really bad moment came when he was away choosing dessert. Old Sister Presgrave, a dragoness who terrorised medical students and all lower forms of nursing life, plumped herself down into Alex's vacant chair and glared at Judy.

'So. I hear you're getting married,' she said without preamble. 'Hmm, about time, if you ask me. That boy of yours needs a father, although it's a pity the real one never came out of the woodwork.'

'Well, I'm out of the woodwork now, Sister Presgrave,' said Alex, appearing at her elbow and smiling sweetly. 'And Judy and I are both very happy to accept your good wishes.'

A look of dawning comprehension and outrage filled Sister Presgrave as she stared up at Alex. She was so stunned by this astonishing titbit of information that she even allowed him to take her arm and help her out of his seat. Then she collected her wits.

'Well, see you treat her a bit better this time than you did before,' she said scathingly.

And with that parting shot, she marched off towards the door. Judy winced as she watched her leave.

'I suppose she'll tell the whole hospital now,' she said ruefully.

'Let her,' said Alex carelessly. 'They'll have to know sooner or later. But never mind about her. What about the people who really matter? Have you told Robin or your parents yet?'

Judy shook her head. 'I thought it would be better for you to spend some more time with Robin first,' she said hesitantly. 'Just so that he can get to know you a bit before we spring it on him. And my parents are coming down for his birthday party at the weekend. Perhaps we can tell them all then.'

'Good idea,' said Alex. 'We'll have two celebrations instead of one.'

But when it came to Saturday afternoon Judy felt more as if she were facing an exam than a party. Her stomach churned nervously as she darted round the kitchen laying out trays of sausage rolls and little cakes. Even after four and a half years, she could not forget the angry scenes that had ensued when she first told her parents that she was pregnant. Her mother had wept while her father raged. They had tried to persuade her to go to the mainland and have the baby adopted, to sue the father for maintenance, to give up medicine and apply for an unmarried mother's allowance. In the heat of their first reaction, they had even told her never to show her face on the farm again. Of course, when Robin was finally born, they had come round, and nothing could have been more generous than their support. Judy was fully aware that she could never have scraped through those difficult years without the occasional cheques from her father. Cheques he could ill afford. All the same, they were hardly likely to welcome Alex with open arms.

The toot of a car horn interrupted her anxious thoughts. Wiping her hands, Judy snatched off her apron and ran outside. Up at the fence she saw Alex carrying a huge carton and whistling cheerfully. Robin was swinging on the gate, but he hastened to open it as his hero approached.

'Is that for me?' he demanded.

'Yes,' agreed Alex, setting down the carton on the path. 'It's a present from your mother. But you're not to open it until the guests come. Right, Judy?'

'Right,' said Judy.

'Do you know what we're having to eat at my party?' asked Robin.

'Well, I don't know what you're having,' replied Alex. 'But I know what I'm having. Leg of boy!'

And he suddenly pounced on his son, tipped him upside-down and carried him, squealing with mingled terror and delight, across the lawn. In no time at all the pair of them were wrestling wildly on the grass, completely careless of mundane problems like stained clothes.

'Alex is good with kids, isn't he?' said Kate, coming up the path to join Judy.

'Yes,' admitted Judy, shaking her head despairingly at the pair on the grass. 'I just hope he's good with parents too. Then this party will really be a success.'

To Judy's relief the party *was* a success. Her parents had had a four-hour drive from their farm near Devonport, and there was no time for anything but the briefest of introductions before the children began to arrive. Judy's father, red-faced and slow-spoken, eyed Alex cautiously but was happy enough to accept a beer from him, while her mother smiled warily and headed for the kitchen. After that it was nothing but chaos as the adults struggled to cope with a dozen four-year-olds playing blind man's buff, spilling jelly on their clothes and bursting into tears whenever their balloons popped. The high point of the afternoon came with the cutting of the cake. When the last strains of 'Happy

Birthday' had died away and Robin had triumphantly blown out the candles, Alex disappeared briefly from the living-room. He came back with the giant carton, now brightly gift-wrapped, and put it into Judy's arms.

'Robin,' he said, 'don't you want to see what your mother's giving you?'

Robin looked up from hacking his way through the birthday cake with a bit of help from Grandmother.

'Yes, please!' he replied enthusiastically. 'But it's really a present from you, isn't it, Alex?'

'No,' said Alex firmly. 'This is from Judy. I had nothing to do with it, except for bringing it in from the car and wrapping it up.'

He looked across at Judy and winked. Judy saw her parents exchange questioning glances, then Robin was down on his knees ripping away at the wrapping paper. He fumbled eagerly with the flaps, and then triumphantly tore them open. Suddenly a great sigh of rapture went up from every child in the room. For an instant Robin sat spellbound, gazing into the box. Then he scrambled to his feet, launched himself at Judy and sprang up, locking his legs around her waist.

'Oh, Mummy, Mummy, thank you!' he cried.

Judy watched with a lump in her throat as Alex helped Robin to lift the wonderful red car out on to the floor. She could never have given Robin such a magnificent present herself— in fact, she wasn't even sure if she approved of such expensive gifts for children—but the look on Robin's face was something she was going to treasure forever.

'I must get a photo of this,' she murmured, moving across to the sideboard where she had left her camera. 'Come on, smile, you two!'

They both looked up at her and grinned. She looked at them through the viewfinder and shook her head slightly with astonishment. They were so much alike, dazzlingly, heart-breakingly alike with their dark hair and brown eyes and perfect teeth. Only a blind person could miss the resemblance. As she clicked the shutter, Judy heard her mother's sudden sharp intake of breath. Well, there was someone who hadn't missed it, she thought grimly. With leaden fingers, she put the camera back on the sideboard, wishing with all her heart that the day was over.

It was five o'clock by the time all the young guests had gone off, clutching balloons and whistles and bags of sweets. There was a tideline of wreckage all around the flat—wrapping paper, burst balloons, spilt popcorn and scattered toys. Robin drove joyfully in and out of the mess, honking his klaxon and shouting, 'B-r-r-o-o-m-m, B-r-r-o-o-m-m!', while Mrs Lacey busily stacked plates and wrapped left-over food. Judy's father was already muttering about the next morning's milking and rattling his car keys, so it was obviously now or never. Judy cast a desperate glance at Alex, took a deep breath and spoke.

'Listen, everyone.'

No response.

'Excuse me,' said Alex. 'Robin, get out of that car for a minute. Nancy, can you stop working, please? George, put your keys away and sit down, will you? Judy and I have something to tell you.'

Robin pouted about being forced out of his car, and had to be consoled with a chocolate frog, while Judy's father grumbled about Saturday night traffic and getting to bed at all hours. Only Mrs Lacey looked pleased, sitting down next to Judy on the couch with her face flushed and excited. She knows, thought Judy. She's guessed. All she's doing now is waiting for Alex to tell her.

But Alex was in no hurry to make his announcement. He strolled across to the refrigerator, drew out a bottle and brought it back to the living-room. From the litter on the dining-table he produced a box which Judy had not even noticed, and drew out five long-stemmed crystal champagne glasses. There was a discreet pop, a wisp of vapour smoked forth, and then Alex poured four glasses of champagne and one of orange soda. He carried them round on a tray and Judy had to bite back a smile as she saw her father handling his glass as gingerly as if it were a live tiger-snake.

'What's all this in aid of, then?' he demanded suspiciously.

Alex paused, holding his glass up to the light, as if he had nothing more on his mind than judging the bouquet of the wine. Judy saw him standing there, arrogant, self-assured, ready to override all opposition, and for a moment she hardly knew whether she loved or hated him. Then he spoke.

'Judy and I are getting married,' he said.

'Now, hang on a minute,' began Mr Lacey in his slow, farmer's voice, 'I've got a few ——'

'Oh, that's wonderful news!' said Mrs Lacey hastily. 'Isn't it, George? I'd like to propose a toast. To Judy and Alex!'

She took a swift gulp of champagne, and Robin obligingly gulped down some orange soda, his eyes darting backwards and forwards over the rim of his glass as he watched the adults.

'I've got a few questions I want answered before I go drinking any toasts,' finished Mr Lacey stubbornly. 'What I want to know is ——'

'I can guess what you want to know,' cut in Alex. 'And I might as well tell you now, I am Robin's father.'

A momentary hush descended on the room. Robin's eyes widened. He drained the last of his orange squash, set the glass down on the floor and padded across to Alex. Then he plucked at Alex's trouser-leg and stared up at him earnestly.

'My real father?' he demanded.

'Yes,' said Alex, his eyes kindling as he looked at the boy.

'Then did you put a seed in my mummy's tummy and make

it grow?' asked Robin in piercing tones.

Mrs Lacey choked on her champagne, Judy closed her eyes and groaned, and Mr Lacey scowled murderously at Alex. Only Alex remained unperturbed.

'Yes,' he said, ruffling Robin's hair. He picked up the child and hugged him, then gazed steadily at his future father-in-law over the little boy's head. 'We were young and stupid and we made a mistake,' he said evenly. 'I've paid for it by missing out on four years of my son's life, and I don't need to tell you what Judy's been through because of it. But that's all over now. We're going to try and straighten things out together. I hope we'll have your blessing, but if not then we'll just have to get along without it, because I intend to marry your daughter anyway. And what you think about it really doesn't matter to me. It's only Judy and Robin who count for me now.'

Mr Lacey stood glaring at Alex for a moment, his mouth set in a grim line and his thatched eyebrows drawn together. Then slowly his fierce expression gave way to a look of grudging respect.

'I reckon I'll drink to that, son,' he said.

And, raising his glass, he proposed the toast.

'To Judy and Alex.'

CHAPTER FOUR

'WELL, here we are,' said Alex. 'Royal Melbourne Children's Hospital. And with a bit of luck we should find Michael somewhere in this rabbit warren.'

Judy followed him in a daze, only half listening as he told her about the excellent facilities and highly trained staff that made it one of the best children's hospitals in the southern hemisphere. As Alex crossed to the reception desk to announce their arrival, Judy sank into a vinyl armchair with a sigh of relief and let the familiar hospital atmosphere wash over her. The smell of disinfectant, the soft pad-pad of nurses' feet as they hurried along the corridors, the sight of a young intern with his stethoscope hanging out of his pocket all seemed wonderfully safe and familiar.

The truth was that she was feeling more than a little intimidated by this visit to Melbourne. First there had been the new experience of flying and, not only that, but flying first class. And then there had been Tullamarine Airport with its gleaming white corridors and vast, pink-tinted windows and one of the Shaws' employees waiting for them with a BMW. After that there was Melbourne itself — huge, smoky and full of the roar of traffic. To Judy, who was island-bred and used to the smell of the sea and the comforting sight of green hills, it came as a shock, and not a very pleasant one. And there was still the ordeal of meeting Alex's parents looming ahead of her. Small wonder that she had jumped at the chance to call in and visit a favourite patient!

'Paging Mr Brewster, paging Mr Brewster. Mr Shaw is waiting for you at the main reception desk.'

It was ten minutes before John Brewster arrived. He was

a large, red-faced man with fair hair carefully combed to conceal a bald patch on his crown, and a neatly trimmed ginger beard. A faint scent of expensive cologne wafted forth as he stepped forward to shake hands with them.

'Alex. Good to see you.'

He turned questioningly towards Judy.

'My fiancée, Dr Judith Lacey.'

They exchanged pleasantries, and then Alex came straight to the point of the visit.

'Well, how is young Michael getting on?' he asked.

The surgeon led them along a corridor and pressed a button for the lift. 'Don't expect too much when you see him,' he cautioned. 'It's only five days since he had surgery, but we're cautiously optimistic. As you no doubt realise, we had to remove other organs with the tumour in order to get it out successfully. We've taken out the spleen and part of the pancreas, and we had to repair the inferior vena cava. But Peter Brooks was here to do that, and he's one of the best vascular surgeons in the business, so the boy couldn't have been in better hands. We had him ventilated post-operatively for two days to help him get over the operation, but he seems to be coming along reasonably well. He's out of Intensive Care and in a paediatric surgical ward now. Ah, here we are! Just along to the left.'

As they entered the cubicle, there was a sudden flurry of movement and a small, dark-haired woman sat up with a start. She pushed back her hair from her face, half rose from her armchair next to the bed, and looked about her with a puzzled expression.

'Oh, I'm sorry, Mr Brewster,' she said. 'I must have dozed off.'

'It's all right, Mrs Burrows,' the surgeon assured her. 'You just sit down and go back to sleep if you possibly can. You look worn out, and we don't want you in here as a patient too.

Now, how's the youngster getting on?'

Judy exchanged a quick greeting with Michael's mother, and then tiptoed over to the bed to look at the boy. He seemed to be dozing in spite of the spaghetti-like coil of tubes that surrounded him. He was being fed intravenously through a drip and had a catheter in his bladder. In addition there was a plastic drain into the operation site. His face seemed pale and waxy-looking, but his breathing was quiet and regular.

'I won't wake him,' whispered Judy, fumbling in her handbag for a wrapped parcel. 'But will you give him this? I know he doesn't like books usually, but he'll probably enjoy this one. It's a joke book.'

'Oh, how kind of you,' said Mrs Burrows softly. 'He'll love that.'

Michael's eyelids fluttered. 'Have you heard the one about the surgeon?' he asked weakly.

'No,' said Judy, mystified.

'He went on a hunting trip for his holiday. When he came back, the nurses said, "How was your holiday?" and the surgeon said "Terrible. I didn't kill a thing. I should have just stayed at the hospital." '

'Michael!' exclaimed his mother in a horrified voice, but the three doctors rocked with laughter.

'He's on the mend,' said Alex, still chuckling. 'We'll have him back terrorising the life out of us at St Thomas's any day now. You just wait and see!'

'Do you really think Michael will recover?' asked Judy later as they sped down the coast road out of Melbourne.

'He should,' said Alex cautiously. 'Unless something happens to set him back. It was a pretty major operation, after all. But he's got the right attitude and that's half the battle. I really admire the kid, lying there telling jokes with all that medical hardware inside him. But this won't do, Judy. We promised ourselves we weren't going to talk shop this weekend.'

'I know,' said Judy, calling her thoughts back to the present with a faint sigh. 'You'd better tell me a bit more about your parents before I meet them.'

'Not nervous, are you?' asked Alex, smiling.

'Nervous? Why should I be nervous?' rejoined Judy, catching his eye and returning the smile 'After all, I fly interstate to stay with millionaires every weekend, surely you realise that? You did say your parents were millionaires, didn't you?'

'Yes,' agreed Alex. 'But don't let it bother you. When they first came out to Australia, they only had ten pounds and two suitcases between them. And, even if they are a bit hard to get on with, they're pretty nice people underneath. They can't wait to meet you.'

'Hard to get on with?' said Judy faintly. 'I'm not sure I like the sound of that. What do you mean—"hard to get on with"?'

Alex grinned, sending tiny laughter-lines crinkling round the corner of his dark eyes, so that Judy longed to reach out and touch him softly on the cheek. He flicked his indicator, glanced over his shoulder and changed lanes with expert control. The engine of the BMW purred contentedly and the needle on the speedometer crept up to ninety kilometres and then a hundred. Outside the car the blue waters of Port Phillip Bay flashed by in the sunlight, and the crowded bungalows were replaced by long belts of luxuriant green trees, broken only by the occasional iron-lace gates of an expensive villa. The sprawling metropolis of Melbourne seemed a million miles away.

'Not far now,' said Alex. 'Sorry, what did you say?'

'Your parents — why are they hard to get on with?'

'Well, my father is the original Russian bear. Great big shoulders, fierce thatched eyebrows, big, loud voice. Loves to bully people and then despises them for giving in to him. But he's got a heart of gold really.'

'Did you say Russian?' demanded Judy incredulously. 'With a name like Shaw?'

'That's right,' agreed Alex. 'His real name was Glazunov. Yuri Glazunov. But he changed it the minute he arrived in Melbourne. Even though he was only a truck driver at first, he always dreamed of owning his own transport company, and he said nobody would ever send cargo with a company whose name they couldn't spell. Shaw was nice and short and snappy, so he chose that instead.'

'What about your mother?' asked Judy curiously. 'Is she Russian too?'

'*Maman*? No, she's French. Aristocratic French of the old school, so she's very keen on duty and etiquette. Her family owned one of the châteaux of the Loire valley. One night in 1941 she went out to a birthday party and came home to find the place had been bombed. The château had gone up in flames and her parents and older brother Gilles were all dead. She was only seventeen, but, instead of taking refuge with relations, she went off and joined the Resistance. During the rest of the war she had an absolutely hair-raising time and wound up in a camp for displaced persons in the Pyrenees. That's where she met my father. And don't ask me how he got there, because I've never really understood it myself. All I know is that he was left behind by the Russian army. I suppose he had dysentery or something.'

'What made them come to Australia?' asked Judy.

Alex shrugged. 'They'd had enough of war,' he said. 'And I think they just wanted to get as far away as possible. Besides, by the time they were accepted as immigrants, they were married and had my two older sisters. They thought Australia would be a good place to bring up a family. You see, my father had ideas of founding a dynasty to inherit his empire — rather like Ivan the Terrible. I'm afraid we've been a grave disappointment to him.'

'In what way?' asked Judy.

'Well, Yvonne started out all right. She married a businessman and they settled in Singapore, where they run the Asian arm of Shaw's. But she doesn't have any children and she's forty-two now. On the other hand Marie-Louise has four kids, but she doesn't know one end of an invoice from the other. She had the bad taste to fall idiotically in love with an impoverished academic, and, to make matters worse, she still is in love with him. So I don't think she's seriously in the race for taking over the great empire of Shaw's when my father retires. And you know about me.'

'What about you?' asked Judy, puzzled.

'Wasting your time messing about in people's guts, when you could be earning money!' bellowed Alex in a heavy Russian accent. 'Is it for this I sent you to Harvard to study business? You'll break your old father's heart, you know!'

'Did he really send you to Harvard to study business?' asked Judy.

'Yes, he did, but my heart wasn't in it. The minute I finished my commerce degree, I was supposed to come tearing back to Melbourne to learn the practical side of the transport industry. Instead I went to Tasmania and enrolled for medicine. He's never really forgiven me. But, anyway, that's all in the past and here we are!'

As he spoke, Alex swung the car into a white gravelled entrance on the seaward side of the road. Judy had a confused impression of high walls and towering elm trees with a fresh green mist of new leaves. Then Alex pressed a button and the car window wound down. He spoke into an intercom set in the wall, and there was a buzzing sound, then the great iron-lace gates in front of them swung open.

'Oh, isn't it beautiful!' exclaimed Judy.

She sat entranced, as the car crept slowly through the gateway. Really it was more like a paradise than a garden, she thought. Flowering peach and cherry trees seemed to pirouette across the sweeping green lawns like ballerinas. Beneath them the ground was starred with fallen petals, and the sunlight cast lacy patterns through their branches. The driveway swung out of sight behind a mass of glossy camellia bushes, and only in the far distance could Judy glimpse the white outline of the house. She twisted eagerly in her seat, anxious to miss nothing, but everywhere she looked was some new wonder. A gazebo, its trellis covered in white flowering vines, an Italian stone bird-bath with a sparrow ruffling its feathers and dipping its beak, a lion-headed fountain, walkways and archways and secluded garden benches, and, everywhere she looked, crowds of tulips, red and gold and purple, nodding their heads in the breeze.

'Oh, slow down, Alex,' she begged. 'It's so pretty.'

He looked at her eager face and smiled. 'You know, Judy, one of the things I like about you is the way your face lights up when you like something,' he said. 'It makes you look good.'

'One of the things?' asked Judy eagerly. 'What else do you like about me?'

'Oh, the way you stay calm and don't flap in emergencies. That was a really neat bit of work you did on that cardiac arrest in Casualty last Tuesday. And you're pretty good at doing sutures too.'

'Oh,' said Judy in a small voice. 'Thanks.'

'Don't mention it. Look, there's *Maman* out on the front porch waiting for us! *Maman, nous voici!*'

He leant out of the car window and gave a piercing whistle. Judy saw the tall, silver-haired woman on the porch break into a smile and come running down the steps with her arms outstretched. Then Alex had brought the car to a careless halt and was racing along the driveway, sending up tiny puffs of dust from the white gravel. They rushed headlong into each other's arms, and Alex swung his mother right off her feet and set her down breathless and laughing on the bottom step. She broke into a torrent of excited French, pinched Alex's ear reprovingly, and then kissed him lovingly on both cheeks.

Judy came hesitantly forward, feeling suddenly shy and wooden. She came from an undemonstrative family and she did not speak French. Besides, now that she had time to examine her, she saw that Alex's mother was alarmingly beautiful and elegant. Mrs Shaw must have been well over sixty, but, apart from her silver hair, she showed no signs of age. Her skin was smooth and olive, and her figure as slender as a twenty-year-old's. And, even to Judy's inexperienced eyes, her tailored emerald suit and white silk blouse looked very, very expensive. The older woman turned away from Alex and moved a few steps along the drive.

'*Maman*, this is Judy! Judy, my mother,' said Alex, following her.

'How do you do, Mrs Shaw?' said Judy, reaching forward to shake hands.

'Call me Celeste,' said the older woman gaily, and, ignoring Judy's outstretched hand, folded her in a scented embrace and kissed her on both cheeks. 'So—you're the mother of my grandson, I hear?'

Judy flushed. 'Yes,' she agreed, stepping back a pace. Celeste's tone was friendly enough, but her dark eyes were searching. Doesn't she believe he's really Alex's son? wondered Judy. And then she almost laughed aloud. Gazing into Celeste's finely sculpted face, she saw the aquiline nose, the wilful mouth and the arrogant lift to the chin that she had seen so often in her own son. One glimpse of Robin would convince her. 'He looks a lot like you,' Judy added.

'Does he?' asked Celeste. And her tone was a mixture of

doubt and grandmotherly excitement. 'Then you must bring him with you next time you come to visit. Now, Alex, bring Judy inside and I'll show her to her room. Your father is busy on the telephone to New York at the moment, but he'll be coming down for dinner. And I beg you, *chéri*, don't say anything to upset him while we're eating. He's been having a great deal of trouble with his ulcer lately, and his doctor says he must stay calm and drink milk. Milk! You can imagine how much notice Yuri takes of that. But at least we must try to avoid any quarrels.'

'I'll behave like a lamb,' Alex promised, winking at Judy. 'Now, just let us get rid of our luggage, and you can take us around the gardens. Judy has been dying to see them properly.'

'Oh, are you fond of flowers?' asked Celeste, her face softening. 'Me, I love them. When we came here this block was nothing but sand and rough grass and gum trees. For years I planned and worked to make it what you see now and it is beautiful, *n'est-ce pas*? It has a rose garden and summer-houses and a lily pond and a herbarium. But I will tell you all about it as we go through them.'

This promising plan was ruined almost as soon as they entered the house. Judy blinked as they left the bright sunshine, and her eyes had barely adjusted enough to let her admire the great gilt mirror and Louis-Quinze occasional table topped with a lavish arrangement of flowers when a door opened and a middle-aged woman in a business suit came out.

'Ah!' said Celeste. 'This is Mrs Thurstans, my husband's personal secretary. She comes down with him whenever he has to leave his Melbourne office. Mrs Thurstans, you know my son Alex, and this is his fiancée, Dr Judith Lacey.'

'How do you do?' said Mrs Thurstans with an apologetic smile. 'Mrs Shaw, I'm sorry to trouble you, but it's about the dinner for the Indonesian Ambassador next Tuesday. We're only expecting thirty-four people since you're holding it at home, but I've just been on to his office and they're planning to include another ten in the official party. Can you possibly come and straighten it out?'

'*Tiens!*' exclaimed Celeste in annoyance. 'Well, Alex, I will just have to leave you to show Judy her room. I'll be with you again as soon as I can, but this may take hours. I'm so sorry.'

Judy followed Alex up the stairs, her darting gaze taking in the luxurious wool carpet, the French Impressionist paintings on the walls and the delicate Venetian glass chandelier that hung from the high ceiling.

'Shouldn't we get our suitcases?' she asked.

'Oh, don't worry. Watkins the handyman has probably brought them up by now,' replied Alex carelessly.

'The house seems huge,' said Judy in an awed voice. 'I should have warned you to give me a ball of string to help me find my way around.'

'What? No sense of direction? I thought you were a bushwalker.'

'I am,' said Judy ruefully. 'But I always take a compass when I'm bushwalking. It is far to our room?'

'Not really,' said Alex. 'Second left, then left again and it overlooks the sea. Oh, by the way, it's your room, not our room. I'm afraid my mother has a strong sense of propriety. But I'm just along the passage.' He led Judy round a couple of quick turnings and then opened a door. 'Here you are,' he said. 'You should get a good view of the sunset from the balcony. And it's close to the pool if you fancy a quick dip in the morning. Good, it looks as though Watkins had his ball of string with him. That's your bag on the bed, isn't it?'

'Yes. Thank you,' said Judy, reaching out to take it from him.

But as he handed her the bag, Alex gave a mutter of annoyance. 'Oh, I'm sorry, Judy. My watch has snagged on your top. Just a minute and I'll get it free.'

The bag slid from her fingers and a faint flush mounted to her cheeks as she watched Alex kneel to disentangle the gold links from the fabric. His fingers were warm and expert, and she yearned to bury her face in his thick dark hair.

'There, it's free!' said Alex. 'But I'm afraid it's left a hole.'

'It doesn't matter,' said Judy hastily. 'It was pretty old.'

She took a quick, sharp breath, overwhelmed by his male nearness. He glanced up at her with a question in his eyes. What he saw seemed to amuse him.

'Pretty old and very unflattering,' he said teasingly. 'Why don't you take it off?'

Before she could protest he had pulled it over her head, sending her chestnut curls tumbling around her face. He smiled at her confusion, then, with a swift movement, undid the catch of her bra and threw that away too. Still kneeling, he buried his face in the warm softness of her breasts. A low moan escaped him.

'Oh, Judy, I want you so badly,' he whispered. Then his hands came firmly round her waist, and he pulled her down towards him.

'Alex, we can't — your mother . . . the door's unlocked,' protested Judy.

'Nothing simpler,' said Alex.

In a couple of strides he had crossed the floor and turned the key in the lock. Before Judy could protest again, she was back in his arms, and his warm kisses were raining down on her face and throat.

'Don't worry about my mother,' he murmured. 'She'll be hours yet.'

With a sigh Judy let herself go and surrendered to the exquisite joy of his caresses. She had never dreamt a man's hands could be so tender and yet so strong. His fingers traced lazy patterns down over her body, and then she let out a tiny gasp as his tongue found her nipple. His lips moved gently, teasingly, and Judy arched her back and pressed herself close against him, feeling as if she were ready to drown with pleasure.

'Mmm,' she murmured, wriggling against him so that she could feel his frantically thudding heart.

'Oh, Judy,' he moaned. Then he caught her to him so hard that he crushed the breath out of her, and they rolled wildly together in a frenzy of kissing.

Just then the phone rang. With a groan Alex shook himself free and sprang to his feet. 'Sorry,' he mouthed at Judy as he picked it up. He held his hand over the receiver. 'It's the internal phone, so if I don't answer it someone is bound to come up.'

She nodded and, feeling suddenly embarrassed by Alex's gaze, bent to pick up her clothes. He sounded annoyed as he spoke into the phone.

'Hello. Alex here. He's what? Well, can't it wait? New York again? Oh, all right, Mrs Thurstans. Tell my father I'll be right down.' He hung up, straightened his tie and strode across to the door. Then, as an afterthought, he came hurriedly back, dropped a brief kiss on Judy's cheek and squeezed her shoulder. 'I'm really sorry about this,' he said. 'Business! But don't worry, I'll catch up with you at dinner.'

As the door slammed, Judy's fingers flew to her cheek, and in the mirror of the great mahogany dressing-table she saw her lips move soundlessly in the words, I love you, Alex. Words she could never say to him, because she knew perfectly well that Alex didn't love her. 'I want you' was all he had said. And, as long as Alex was no more than cool and friendly, her pride would not allow her to show what she felt for him. Although he hadn't exactly been cool a moment ago, she thought with a swift reminiscent smile. Sometimes she felt that, if only they could be alone together long enough, Alex's teasing affection for her might blossom into love. But at home there was always Robin to interrupt them, and here there were the demands of Shaw's International Transport Company. Shaw's! thought Judy indignantly, as she hauled on her clothes. Did business and money run everybody's life in this household? She looked at herself critically in the mirror. In despite of her flushed cheeks and rumpled hair, she really was quite pretty, she thought. Not beautiful like Stephanie Hargreaves, but pretty enough. Her spirits lifted. Alex would be beside her soon, and with luck the ordeal of her first dinner with his parents would go off well.

In fact, the dinner was a disaster. To begin with, it was much later than Judy had expected. By the time the gong rang at eight o'clock, she was starving, but when she entered the dining-room only Celeste was there.

'I'm sorry, my dear,' she apologised. 'Yuri and Alex are still talking business, but they shouldn't be long. Let me get you another sherry while we're waiting.'

'Thank you,' said Judy.

Her glance travelled miserably over Celeste's smart after-five dress of black crêpe with tiny diamanté clips at the cuffs. Judy was still wearing her simple skirt and knitted top with the snag marks from Alex's watch. I wish I'd changed, she thought, but was uncomfortably conscious that nothing in her suitcase upstairs would have passed Celeste's scrutiny. She took a deep breath and told Celeste how beautiful the room was. Half an hour dragged by as Celeste talked knowledgeably of Sèvres china and Bruges lace and the château where she had grown up. They had just moved on to discussing the Tasmanian dairy farm where Judy had grown up when the door opened and Yuri and Alex walked in.

It was clear at once that they had been quarrelling. Yuri's face was set in a thunderous scowl and Alex's dark eyes blazed with anger. Celeste moved between them, casting her son a reproachful look.

'Yuri,' she said swiftly, 'you must meet Alex's fiancée, Judy. And do stop clutching that telephone, I beg you. It's time we sat down to dinner.'

'Hmmph,' responded Yuri, transferring the telephone to his left hand so that he could shake hands with Judy. He looked for all the world like a giant child determined not to give up a toy, and Judy's eyes danced as she rose to greet him.

'Something amuses you?' asked Yuri, looking down at her slender fingers engulfed in his giant paw.

'Oh, no,' Judy hastened to assure him.

'You don't look old enough to have a four-year-old child, and you're very thin,' he said, looking at her critically. 'I always thought my son preferred women who had something to get hold of.'

This brought a muffled explosion of laughter from Alex and a shocked reproof from Celeste, but Judy simply grinned, not in the least offended. Without waiting for a reply, Yuri lowered himself into his seat.

'All the same, I'm glad to see he's settling down at last,' he said. 'You wouldn't believe what I've been through with that boy, the money I've spent on him. And how does he repay me? Does he come and work in the company I built up with my own sweat all these years? No, he becomes a doctor. A doctor! Do you know what I think of doctors?'

'No,' said Judy.

'Quacks, the lot of them. Only good at one thing—taking your money and giving you a lot of rubbishy advice. Do you know what my doctor tells me? Eat slowly, drink milk, lose weight and don't take your business troubles home with you. Me, the chairman of Shaw's! The man's a fool! All right,

Celeste, I understand sign-language. I'll be quiet as soon as I get something to eat. What sort of pap are you serving me up tonight? Baby food? Porridge?'

Neither of these dismal items appeared on the menu. In fact, the food was excellent. First a grilled fillet of trevally with a delicate cream sauce, followed by a carbonade of beef with puréed potatoes and lightly steamed vegetables, and finally a dessert of crème caramel. But Judy found it almost impossible to enjoy the delicacies set in front of her. Three times during the main course Yuri's telephone rang and he launched into complicated business discussions, which made his face turn redder and his voice grow louder each time. And then, just after the coffee was brought in, the final crisis erupted. The long-awaited call from New York arrived.

It was obvious that things were not going to Yuri's satisfaction. He leapt out of his seat and strode around the dining-room, waving his free hand and shouting into the phone. The New York agent was a fool, his staff were a lot of snivelling no-hopers, and they couldn't transport a paper bag across a kitchen floor. What was more, if the problem wasn't solved within one hour, they could all look for jobs elsewhere. By the time Yuri hung up, his face had turned alarmingly purple and he was panting slightly. With a faint groan he flung the telephone down on the dining-table, pressed his fingers to his midriff and looked angrily round the room for a scapegoat. He found it in his son.

'This is all your fault,' he accused. 'If you had come to Melbourne and taken over as chairman, the way I've been begging you to for the last five years, I wouldn't have to put up with this sort of thing. And why won't you do it? Because you're plain stubborn. It's not as though I don't offer you enough. Only this afternoon, I said to you, "Alex, now that you're getting married, forget all this medical rubbish and I'll build you a nice house right here next to us on the Bay and you can take over everything as Shaw's. I'll give you half a million dollars a year, and I'll double your present shareholding." And what did you say to me? "No," that's what you said. "No"! I just don't understand it. What do you earn as a doctor, anyway? Fifty thousand a year? A hundred thousand? I'll pay you ten times that amount. But you've no respect for a poor old man. All you want to do is waste your time messing around with people's guts. You're totally selfish, and you don't care if you kill me with overwork!'

Alex opened his mouth to reply, intercepted a look from Celeste, and clamped his lips angrily shut. But Judy would not be so easily silenced. She leapt to her feet, her eyes sparkling.

'That's completely unfair!' she exclaimed. 'Alex is a wonderful doctor, and he certainly doesn't waste his time! There was a little girl brought in from a road accident only two weeks ago needing brain surgery. Everyone expected her to die on the operating table, but Alex saved her, and now she's making a total recovery. I don't see how you can possibly put a price on that kind of thing. And, as for killing you with overwork, anyone can see that you're killing yourself. How you can expect people to respect you when you're silly enough to abuse your body the way you do is beyond me! Anyway, Alex is thirty-two years old, and I think he's entitled to live his own life. Excuse me!'

With a little sob of anger, Judy flung down her lace-edged table napkin and stormed out of the room. Her eyes were blurred and her pulses racing, but by the time she reached the long picture gallery upstairs her rage had cooled enough to make her realise what she had done. To her surprise, she found she had taken a wrong turning and was in an unfamiliar part of the house, with the corridor in front of her coming to a dead end at a window overlooking the Bay. She twitched back the curtain and looked at the dark water below her, hearing the faint whispering noise it made as the waves broke on the sandy beach. How could I have been so rude? she thought, appalled at the memory of what she had said. A faint groan escaped her as she realised she would have to go back and apologise.

'Are you feeling unwell?' asked a familiar voice behind her.

Judy swung round. 'Celeste! Oh, I'm so sorry! It was unpardonable of me. I must go down and apologise.'

'Tt! Tt! Not now,' said Celeste with a twinkle in her eye. 'Yuri has had quite enough excitement for one evening, and, in any case, you only said what I was dying to say myself. Now, why don't you come into my private sitting-room with me and we'll have a little chat?'

The room which Celeste ushered her into was very prettily furnished with gold brocade armchairs, a gold carpet and richly textured white wallpaper. A huge gilt mirror dominated one wall.

'Do sit down,' Celeste invited, 'and I'll make you some fresh coffee. I keep a percolator here, and I always come up to enjoy a second cup after dinner. There's no phone in this room, you see.'

Judy sank gratefully into the comfort of a striped sofa, and watched the older woman's deft movements as she prepared the coffee.

'I really am sorry about what happened downstairs,' she confessed. 'I honestly didn't intend to have a big quarrel with Alex's father on my first day here.'

'Oh, my dear!' exclaimed Celeste. 'That wasn't a big quarrel. For Yuri that was nothing more than a little skirmish. I try to keep things calm for him, but it's really just a waste of time. And, you know, I must make an apology to you too.'

'To me?' asked Judy in bewilderment. 'What on earth for?'

Celeste gave a wry smile. 'For doubting your motives in marrying Alex,' she said frankly. 'Such a lot of girls have pursued him over the years for the sake of his money that I was afraid you were doing the same thing. But I saw tonight that I was wrong. Money means nothing to you, *n'est-ce pas*? I also saw something else tonight, which made me very happy.'

'What was that?' asked Judy, puzzled.

'That you are in love with my son. And I hope, Judy, that if I tell you I am now very pleased that you and Alex are getting married, you will allow me to ask you a most impertinent question.'

'Yes?' said Judy warily.

'Is your son really Alex's child?'

Judy did not answer for a moment. Then, by way of reply, she took off the gold locket which was her only jewellery and passed it to Celeste.

'Look inside,' she said huskily. 'It's a photo of Robin taken last Christmas.'

Celeste took the locket and snapped it open. For several seconds, she was silent, gazing at it. Then she shook her head in disbelief. 'He is the image of Alexander,' she said in a voice full of emotion. 'Wait, wait. I have a photo somewhere here in one of these albums.' She rummaged in a mahogany cupboard and hauled out a pile of leather covered albums. 'No, not that one, that's the migrant camp. And those are Yvonne's baby photos. Look, here it is! Now, aren't they just identical?'

She sat down beside Judy and their heads bent together over the photos.

'Oh, look at this one!' cried Judy. 'What on earth is he doing here?'

'Oh, the little monster!' exclaimed Celeste. 'You would not believe what a naughty child he was! I had invited some friends over for afternoon tea, and I locked him out of the dining-room so he would not touch the cakes before they came. He was so bad, he climbed on to the roof of the garage and got in through a window. I found him there all covered in chocolate, just as you see. Only three years old, just imagine it!'

'Robin's like that too,' Judy agreed sympathetically.

'Ah, yes. Alex gets his looks from me, but his—how do you say it in English?—his pigginess comes from Yuri.'

'Pig-headedness, I think you mean,' said Judy with a gurgle of laughter.

'Exactly!' agreed Celeste. 'Now, how do you like your coffee?'

'White, please, one sugar. Do you mind if I look at the rest of these photos?'

'No, no, go ahead,' invited Celeste.

They sat companionably together on the sofa, browsing through the albums and laughing. By the time they had finished the coffee, the pictures of Alex as a mischievous child had given way to snapshots of Alex as an adult. Alex playing his guitar, Alex in a miner's helmet and khaki overalls deep in the bowels of a cave, Alex with a stethoscope around his neck. Then Judy turned a page and the laughter died out of her face. In front of her was a glossy enlargement of Alex with a rapturous smile on his face, and his arm lovingly around Stephanie Hargreaves.

'Now, that was one of the girls who was after Alex only for his money,' said Celeste disapprovingly. 'I was glad when they broke up, even though Alex was so upset about it. She was a very beautiful girl, but quite heartless.'

'I know,' agreed Judy miserably.

'You knew her?' asked Celeste in surprise.

Judy nodded. ' But I've never really understood what happened,' she said. ' Alex told me she left him for someone rich, but why should she? I know the rest of us didn't realise Alex was wealthy, but she must have known it, surely? After all, they were engaged.'

'Oh, yes, *chérie*, she knew it,' replied Celeste bitterly. 'But Alex obviously hasn't told you what happened. When he left for Canada, he and Yuri were in the middle of one of their worst conflicts ever. Yuri told Alex he would cut him off without a rouble if Alex didn't give up medicine, and Alex said he wouldn't take any of Yuri's money anyway. When Alex announced to Stephanie that they would have to live on his salary as a doctor, she very soon found that she was in love with somebody else. Somebody richer.'

'I see,' said Judy in a small voice. 'But Alex is still in love with her, isn't he?'

'Oh, my poor child,' said Celeste, putting the photo album down on the coffee-table and taking Judy's hands in hers. 'So that is what is troubling you, then?'

Judy looked into those warm brown eyes and found she could not deny it. She nodded, trying to swallow the painful lump in her throat.

'I'm sure he will make you a good husband,' said Celeste encouragingly. 'You know, among the people I grew up with, there were many of these *mariages de convenance*, and some of them were very happy.'

'I know,' said Judy, blinking. 'It's just that——'

'You want something more?'

'Yes,' agreed Judy.

'Men are such fools!' exclaimed Celeste, rising to her feet and walking across to the mirror. 'Still, one cannot altogether blame him. She was so beautiful, and always so charming and well dressed.' She stopped dead, with an arrested look on her face. Her glance travelled sharply over Judy's clothes. 'Judy!' she commanded. 'Come here!'

Judy walked over to her with a puzzled expression, and found herself being thrust in front of the mirror, with her hair held in bunches framing her face.

'Just as I thought!' exclaimed Celeste triumphantly. 'A little make-up, a new hairstyle, the right clothes and *voilà*! Tomorrow, *ma petite*, you and I are going shopping! And, you'll see, this is one marriage of convenience which will turn out very well!'

It was nearly sunset on the following day when Judy came nervously down the steps from the patio to the swimming-pool. Alex was standing at the other end and she watched his lean, tanned body appreciatively as he curved over and then dived. He churned through the water with powerful strokes until he had covered ten laps. Then he came to a halt, panting and laughing, and called to her to bring him a towel. She picked it up and walked along to him, conscious of her new hairstyle, the faint scent of Arpège that rose from her body, and the stylish pleated skirt and blazer that Celeste had chosen for her. Alex took the towel from her with a grateful smile and buried his face in it. Then slowly he raised his head. An expression of astonishment came over him.

'Judy,' he said in amazement, 'what have you done? You look gorgeous.'

Judy grinned, not even bothering to protest as he gathered her into his arms and the chlorinated water dripped all over her beautiful new suit. After all, Shaw's International Transport Company could afford it, and she was beginning to think that Celeste might be right. Perhaps this was one marriage of convenience which would work out very well.

CHAPTER FIVE

THEY were married in an old stone church in Battery Point on a day full of sunshine and showers and the scent of spring gardens. Forever after, the events of her wedding-day remained in Judy's mind like a series of wonderful snapshots. Early in the morning there was herself, dressed in ivory satin, with a wreath of blue and white hyacinths in her hair and Alex's emeralds sparkling on her finger. She gazed and gazed at herself in the old spotted glass of the wardrobe mirror and could scarcely believe it was all true. But the empty room with just a couple of cartons taped up and waiting to be collected told its own story.

Afterwards there was a gleaming dark limousine with a uniformed chauffeur, courtesy of Shaw's, to whisk her away to the church, and then just enough time for a last-minute check on the sandstone steps. By this time she had butterflies in her stomach, no question about it—Blue Emperors, probably! she thought—but the sight of her father calmed her down. He looked so proud and delighted, standing there twisting his finger in the neck of his starched shirt. And Robin was absolutely adorable as a page-boy in red velvet, until Judy turned him round and made a horrible discovery—'Kate! He's got *earthworms* in his back pocket, the little wretch!'—and Kate herself was ravishing in a red bridesmaid's dress. Then suddenly the deep voice of the organ sounded from the church's interior and Judy felt everything go still and solemn inside her.

She could feel herself trembling with joy as she walked down the aisle on her father's arm, turning slightly to acknowledge the smiles from her friends. Half of St Thomas's hospital seemed to be packed into the church, but the one person who mattered most was standing at the end of the nave and waiting for her. As he turned towards her, Judy felt her heart leap. Oh, Alex, she thought. Love me. Please. But his face was brooding and inscrutable, and for a moment a tremor of doubt shot through her. Then his expression lightened and he winked at her. His lips curved into a grin and she smiled back at him radiantly. The bridal march died away and the vicar stepped forward to begin the service.

Later, with a gold wedding band firmly on her finger and Alex's kiss still tingling on her lips, she sat through the reception and wondered blissfully whether she had ever been so happy in her life. All the people she loved best were there. Mum and Dad and her brother Jim, all a bit overawed by the grandeur of the hotel, Robin with his lace cravat dangling in his soup, Yuri holding up a large glass of milk and toasting the bride extravagantly in Russian, and Celeste, as elegant as the centrefold from a Vogue magazine. Not to mention their friends. Everyone from Alex's anaesthetist Richard Pryor to the businesslike Mrs Thurstans was present. The only one missing is Mr Ossi, thought Judy, smiling.

But when she came outside in a tailored green suit at the end of the reception, she found that Kate and Richard had arranged even that. Lying on the back seat of the BMW, impeccably attired in a pin-striped morning suit with a white carnation in his buttonhole and a bottle of Veuve Clicquot clutched in his bony hand, was the skeleton himself. Judy dissolved in helpless giggles, and it was left to Alex to get rid of the unwanted passenger, untie all the old boots and cans dangling from the bumper bar, and get them both safely to the airport. All the way through the flight to New Zealand, she remained wrapped in a dream, and it was not until sunset that she finally emerged from it.

They were standing on the shores of Milford Sound, watching the last rays of the sun glowing on the water, with the cliffs soaring dramatically above them. Alex's hand was resting casually on her shoulder, and she tilted her cheek so that it lay against his warm fingers.

'Pinch me,' she invited.

'What for?'

'It's all so beautiful, I can't believe it's real.'

'We'll soon fix that,' said Alex cheerfully.

'Ow. I believe you. It's real! It's real!'

'I can think of a better way of convincing you,' he said.

And his lips came down fresh and persuasive on hers. There was no longer any reason to resist him, and her mouth opened slowly and sweetly against his. She sighed and nestled deeply into his arms, feeling the steady beating of his heart against her. Then she lifted her hand to touch his thick, dark hair, and the sun sent a gleam of light darting off the gold band on her finger. A little thrill of happiness went through her. It was true. She and Alex were finally married.

'Real enough for you, Mrs Shaw?' asked Alex teasingly.

She nodded, too overcome to speak, but her eyes glowed. Alex looked down at her intently and a pang went through him. Mrs Shaw. He had hoped one day to say those words to Stephanie. For a moment the vision of her turbulent blonde hair, her huge violet eyes and her perfect smile flashed before him. Then he gazed down and saw Judy instead. Feisty little Judy, with her sparkling green eyes and determined chin. Judy, who could raise a baby single-handed, get a medical degree and have a blazing row with his formidable old father. His face softened.

'Come on,' he said. 'How about a big dinner of New Zealand lamb, and an hour or so on the dance-floor? We're on our honeymoon, remember?'

They had little chance to forget it during the next week. Both of them were determined to make the most of this rare chance

for a holiday, and they crammed every daylight hour full of
bushwalking and sightseeing, wining and dining and
dancing. The nights proved even more magical, for to Judy's
relief there was a strong physical chemistry between them
which seemed to affect Alex just as powerfully as her. They
had started out the week as virtual strangers, but by the time
they had to leave they were accomplices in love. A whole
language of looks and smiles and caresses now bound them
together. And, even though she was beginning to miss Robin
desperately, Judy was quite sorry when the time came to go
home.

'Oh, well. Back to reality!' she said with a sigh as New
Zealand disappeared under the wing-tip of the plane.

It was back to reality with a vengeance when they returned
to the wards. Judy was no stranger to exhaustion, but the life
of a hospital intern had never seemed more tiring. Monday
to Friday she was hard at work nine hours a day. That didn't
worry her—in fact she thrived on it—but it was the time she
had to spend on call that was really difficult. Three nights a
week she slept at the hospital, and what had been awkward
when she lived in Kate's downstairs flat became downright
impossible. On their return from their honeymoon, Alex's
father had surprised them with the gift of a 'nice little house
in a decent suburb'. The nice little house had eleven rooms,
a swimming-pool, half an acre of garden, was miles away
from the hospital, and really needed a full-time staff of three
just to keep it going. When she pointed this out anxiously to
Alex, he simply shrugged. 'Hire some help,' he said, as if that
solved everything.

But hiring help only seemed to add to Judy's problems. The
first housekeeper/nanny sent by the employment agency was
an intimidating dragon of a woman called Mrs Henderson, who
cooked boiled tripe and had a foolproof method of dealing with

children who were picky eaters. You simply served the same lot of food up until it finally disappeared. On the fifth day of her reign Robin's boiled tripe and cabbage finally disappeared—down the lining of her nice new tartan shopping bag. Mrs Henderson disappeared the same day. She was succeeded by a Mrs O'Hara, who cleaned the house beautifully and cooked nourishing, if rather stodgy meals, but after three weeks went out one evening 'for a bit of a flutter at the Casino' and did not reappear for nearly a week. When Judy summoned up the courage to dismiss her, she demanded a month's wages and departed with an air of indignation, leaving behind her a strong aroma of brandy and a dresser drawer full of empty bottles. At this point Judy fought down an overpowering temptation to have hysterics, and simply told Alex quietly that she would rather manage without any help in the house. He was surprised, but perfectly willing to agree. 'Whatever you want, Judy,' he said kindly. 'You know I leave the household management entirely up to you.'

I certainly do, Judy thought grimly in the days that followed, as she struggled to keep up with the endless cooking, cleaning and ironing that marriage seemed to entail. Gone were the days of eating baked beans on toast with Robin in the kitchen, and wearing non-iron polyester clothes hastily snatched off the clothesline to work. Alex had been brought up surrounded by wealth and luxury. He expected high standards of food and clothing as a matter of course, but seemed to be maddeningly unaware of the work involved in maintaining them. Occasionally, to her astonishment, Judy found herself yearning for the simplicity of life back in her tiny Battery Point flat, with Kate always upstairs ready to babysit or gossip at a moment's notice and the shops just around the corner.

All the same, there were good times too. Long walks at the Botanical Gardens with Alex and Robin wrestling on the sunlit lawns, a couple of rowdy evenings at the folk club, where they discovered a common liking for the Chieftains, a day's bushwalking at Mount Field amid the sound of rushing water and the strange primeval gloom of the fern glades. There were good moments at the hospital too, like the day when they worked frantically together to resuscitate a child who had almost drowned, or the times Judy assisted Alex in the operating theatre. At moments like that they were a team, labouring together almost like a single heart and brain and pair of hands. There were tragedies and triumphs to share. Judy wept soundlessly into Alex's shoulder one night after a child road-trauma victim slipped silently from coma into death. And she shared his joy when Michael Burrows, weak and pale but still cracking jokes, was finally allowed to go home.

But most of the time Judy's life seemed to be nothing more than a blur of exhaustion, a constant frantic struggle to cope with admitting patients, stitching up drunks, groping her way out of bed to deal with 3 a.m. cardiac arrests, and coping with all the mundane things as well. There were plenty of those. Getting Robin out of bed early enough to bathe and feed him and drop him off at Kate's before work, going to the supermarket, washing, cooking, cleaning, and always, always trying to stay cheerful about it all. Always on her best behaviour, trying to keep Alex happy. Trying to make the marriage work.

It was about a month after the departure of Mrs O'Hara when it all came unstuck. Judy had overslept by fifteen minutes and Robin, who seemed to have a radar system that told him when she was busiest, was deliberately dawdling in the bath and splashing water over the side with the force of a tidal wave. Alex, who was already shaved and dressed, sat at the dining-table, leafing through a copy of *Lancet*.

'Some French toast would be nice for breakfast,' he called through to the kitchen. 'And perhaps a bit of bacon—if it's not too much trouble.'

'Of course not,' cried Judy hysterically, flinging clothes into the washing-machine, snatching up a mop and bucket and heading for the bathroom. 'I'll just get Robin out of the bath first.'

By the time she had dragged Robin kicking and squealing out of the bath, dried him, dressed him and dropped him in front of the television set, Alex was drumming his fingers on the dining-table and casting occasional hopeful glances at the kitchen stove. Judy swept past in her dressing-gown, rummaged furiously in the fridge, and then set some bacon under the grill before sprinting off to get dressed. When she returned the bacon was colouring nicely, filling the room with its savoury fragrance. Hurriedly she set a frying-pan on the range and began breaking the eggs into a bowl. Twenty-two minutes to eight. She could still do it, but only just. Professor Castle, the head of the clinical school, hated people to be late, and she was sure he was waiting to catch her out. The French toast went into the pan and, with a sigh of relief, Judy sat down at the kitchen table and closed her eyes. Nineteen minutes to. If only Robin would eat quickly, she'd be fine . .
.

The next thing she knew was the strong smell of smoke filling the kitchen and Robin's shrill voice shrieking excitedly. She opened her eyes and blinked, looking around in horror.

'The kitchen's on fire! The kitchen's on fire! Mummy, Daddy! The kitchen's on fire!'

Before she could even move, Alex had rushed in to the rescue. He picked up the frying-pan, swore as it burnt his fingers, snatched at it again with an oven glove, then flung it into the sink. There was a mighty sizzle as cold water from the tap hit the hot metal and a cloud of steam hissed up into the air. Robin let out another yell of fear or excitement.

'Be quiet, Robin!' said Alex irritably. 'There's no need to

make such a fuss.'

'But the kitchen's on fire!' bellowed Robin.

'No, it isn't! exclaimed Alex. 'It was just the frying-pan, see? I'll lift you up and show you.'

Robin inspected the congealed black mess in the frying-pan, then turned to Judy and scowled.

'You've burnt my French toast!' he said severely.

'Never mind about that now,' warned Alex. 'You'd better go and get in the car or we'll be late for work.'

'But I haven't had my breakfast!'

Robin's voice was swelling with indignation. Any minute now, thought Judy wearily, and he'll fling himself on the floor and throw a massive tantrum, which is all I need. She made a small sound in her throat, half groan, half sigh. Alex's gaze swung sharply round to her and then stopped, as if he were seeing her for the very first time. She shifted restlessly under that scrutiny, miserably aware of her pale cheeks, her rumpled hair, the shadows under her eyes. Miserably aware also of the dismay which suddenly filled her husband's face as he stared at her.

'How did it happen?' he asked abruptly.

'I—I don't really know,' she confessed, brushing a tendril of hair out of her eyes. 'I think I fell asleep.'

'Asleep——?' asked Alex incredulously.

But before Judy could begin to explain, Robin interrupted.

I want my breakfast!' he yelled.

Both adults jumped, but Alex was first to recover.

'Blow your breakfast, you little brat!' he snapped. 'Go and sit in the car before I really get angry with you.'

Robin's bottom lip quivered, and he trailed sadly across to the back door, casting them both a reproachful glance. Alex relented a little.

'You can take a banana to eat on the way,' he suggested.

Robin brightened. 'Will I turn into Banana Man and fly

away?' he asked.

'We can always hope . . .' murmured Judy, her voice brimming with amusement. But the laughter died out of her eyes as she caught Alex's gaze. He was scowling angrily, and his lips were pressed together in the thin line that usually promised trouble for some unfortunate nurse.

'Alex, w—what's the matter?' she faltered.

He looked down at his watch and gave an impatient sigh.

'It's impossible,' he said. 'We just can't go on like this—it's not working. But there's no use trying to discuss it at the moment. We'll both be late if we don't get moving. When do you finish today?'

'Five-thirty.'

'All right. I'll pick you up and we'll go out somewhere. I'm operating this afternoon, so I'll be at St Thomas's anyway. I only hope I'm not stuck with some fool of an assistant surgeon who doesn't know one end of a scalpel from another.'

'Actually, it's me,' said Judy in a small voice.

'What's you?'

'The fool of an assistant surgeon. I'm rostered to help you this afternoon.'

'Oh, lord,' said Alex. 'Are you really? Well, I'm sorry I said that. No offence meant—you were perfectly competent the last time you worked with me. But try and stay awake, will you? There's a good girl.'

Judy's feeling were in turmoil all the way into town. Alex didn't speak, but concentrated all his attention on driving, changing lanes and waiting at traffic lights with a controlled tension that only intensified her panic. What on earth had he meant? She struggled to recall his exact words. 'We just can't go on like this—it's not working.' Was he trying to tell her their marriage was over? How would she bear it? She stole a glance at him, hoping for reassurance, for a smile or one of his friendly winks, but there was nothing. Only a cold, stern profile that might have been chiselled out of marble.

All morning she trailed around the wards with a bright, artificial smile frozen on her face and her heart aching. She marvelled at the way she was able to take down admission details for an elderly asthmatic, soothe a nervous old lady about to have a plaster removed, and discuss a diagnosis with a thoracic surgeon, without yielding to the urge to burst into tears and rush out of the hospital. Time seemed to have stopped, and more than once she glanced up at the ward clock, convinced that her watch was not working. She both dreaded and longed for two o'clock, when she would see Alex again, but knew it would do her no good to see him. By the time she wandered into the cafeteria at one-thirty she looked so miserable that two of her fellow interns, David Carstairs and Matthew Parker, took it on themselves to cheer her up. They whisked her off to their table, bought her an orange juice, told her Irish jokes, and laid extravagant bets about which one of them would be first to take out the gorgeous new blonde nurse on Paediatrics. Judy just smiled wanly and went on pushing a piece of wilted lettuce around her plate. Then, at ten to two, she laid down her knife and fork and went off with a face like a martyr.

'Marriage doesn't seem to be doing her much good,' commented David, shaking his head as he watched her go.

'It's probably not marriage that's the problem,' said Matthew. 'I reckon she's just shaking in her shoes at the thought of assisting old Shaw in theatre. I know I was.'

'Yeah. He's a real ogre, isn't he? Good surgeon, though. Still, I hope he's not giving her a hard time.'

Alex was giving Judy a hard time. He was in one of the moods which the theatre sister recognised and dreaded. Full of brisk, curt commands, and ready to turn to biting sarcasm if these were not instantly obeyed. Sister Anne Watson was a motherly, middle-aged soul with twenty years of marriage behind her, and could well imagine the strain of assisting a surgeon who was not only in an unpleasant mood, but was also one's husband. She did not miss the tense expression on Judy's face, or the quick, nervous glance she cast the surgeon as she scrubbed up. Poor little thing, thought Sister Watson indignantly. I'll make her a nice cup of tea when they finish this op and spoil her a bit. And I won't let him upset her between patients either.

The result was that each time Judy came into the coffee-room between operations, hoping for a quick word with Alex, she found herself thwarted. Either somebody else would be in there talking, or, if the room was miraculously empty of anaesthetists and nurses, Sister Watson would instantly materialise. At last, just before the final operation of the afternoon, Judy came along from the recovery-room and found Alex alone. He looked up with a faint lightening of his frown as she entered, but before Judy could speak Sister Watson popped her head around the door and smiled brightly at her.

'Oh, there you are, Dr Shaw. Shall I make you a nice cup of tea? It doesn't give you much time, does it, when you have to write up the operation notes between patients? Now, how do you like it? Milk and one sugar? Here we are.'

'Thank you,' said Judy, taking the cup and sitting down.

Alex had buried himself in a magazine, and he remained buried as Sister Watson sat down and chatted about what she was buying her children for Christmas, where she was planning to go for her summer holidays, and how shocking the price of meat was these days. But, before she could expand on these themes, a nurse appeared in the doorway.

'Telephone, Sister Watson,' she said.

Judy leant anxiously forward and glanced around, unable to bear the uncertainty any longer.

'Alex, about what happened this morning——' she began nervously.

He flung down the magazine and looked directly at her, his dark eyes troubled. For a moment he seemed about to speak, and he lifted his hands expressively, then dropped them back into his lap.

'Oh, what's the point?' he said bitterly. 'I thought I was doing the right thing, you know, but it's just not working out. You see——'

'Alex, are you trying to tell me——'

'Oh, Mr Shaw, your next patient is ready now. It's that little boy for the appendicectomy.'

Sister Watson's cheerful tones cut ruthlessly into their discussion. She consulted her clipboard and stole a glance at the pair of them. Just as well she'd come in, by the look of things, she reflected. You could cut the atmosphere in here with a knife.

'James Harvey,' she added.

Judy's feet felt like lead as she followed Alex back along the corridor to the theatre. There's no doubt about it now, she thought gloomily. He wants a divorce. 'I thought I was doing the right thing . . . but it's just not working out.' Well, it was decent of Alex to try. Lots of men would have just disappeared into the wild blue yonder the moment they learnt they had a child. At least now Robin would carry Alex's name, would have someone to call his father, even if they weren't going to be together any longer. But the thought of Alex packing up and leaving affected her so powerfully that she had to stifle a sob in her throat.

'Are you all right?' asked Alex.

'Yes, of course,' said Judy hastily.

But, all the time she was scrubbing up, she kept darting miserable glances at him. It was all so silly. Why should he leave her just because she burnt the breakfast one morning? But it wasn't about the breakfast, she reminded herself, scrubbing savagely at her nails with the sterile brush. It was really about everything else. Like the fact that he didn't love her. Sighing, she walked away from the sink and into the theatre, and stood patiently while the assistant nurse did up her gown. A pang of conscience went through her. She must stop thinking about Alex and concentrate on the patient.

But the moment she was gowned and gloved, the discipline of habit took over. She went and stood at the child's left side and watched while Sister Watson handed Alex a bowl of iodine and a swab. And when Alex had draped the patient and clipped the towels in place, she felt the familiar eager alertness rise up inside her, so that she was instantly ready to obey all his commands. Without hesitation, she swabbed away the blood after the incision was made, and held the wound apart with retractors. There was no doubt about Alex's skill. She watched attentively as he delivered the appendix, clipped the arteries, and tied them in a few deft movements. The moment Judy had cut the ligatures he was back at work, clipping the appendix, tying and cutting it and calling for catgut to suture the stump. Almost before she knew it, they were at the final stages of the operation and Alex was closing the wound with chromic catgut, while Judy stood by ready to cut the sutures as they were tied. A few more minutes and it was all safely over. Judy straightened up with a sigh, as she watched Jamie being wheeled out of the theatre.

'You sound as if you're ready for a rest,' said Sister Watson.

'I certainly am,' said Judy. 'I'll just get out of my gown and write up the operation notes, and then I'm off.'

She was in the recovery-room, staring at Jamie's form and fiddling aimlessly with her biro, when Alex came in. His warm hand rested for a moment on her shoulder. 'Ready, Dr Kildare?' he asked.

Her gaze flew up to meet his, and he was puzzled by the expression which flitted across her face. Amusement? Pleasure? Dismay? It seemed to be all of them at once. He was suddenly curious to know what she was really thinking and feeling. Most of the time it did not even occur to him to wonder, but there was something about Judy, a mischievous sparkle that lurked around her eyes and the corner of her mouth, which all too often fled when he talked to her. It happened now, as her features settled back into a bland mask. Alex felt provoked, almost excited by it. It's time I got to know you, my lady, he thought—high time. And, as always when he was thinking deeply, his brow furrowed into a scowl of concentration.

'I'll just get my bag,' said Judy breathlessly, unnerved by his relentless frown.

'Did you get a babysitter?' asked Alex.

'Yes. Kate was working in the library today, but she's picking Robin and Tamsin up from the crèche when she gets off at six. She'll take him back to her place.'

'Good. Well, do you feel like something to eat? I know it's rather early for dinner, but I'm starving.'

Within twenty minutes they were seated in the courtyard of a restaurant in Salamanca Place. The building was a converted warehouse, and the thick sandstone walls built by the early convicts shut out all the noise of the docks outside. Indeed, it could hardly have been more peaceful. Although it was nearly six o'clock, the sun was still streaming down on to the creeper-clad walls and the tubs of flowers arranged against them. Bees buzzed lazily among the tangles of marigolds and blue lobelias, and the air was perfumed with the sweet scent of honeysuckle. High up in the cloudless blue sky a pair of seagulls flew, shrieking and swooping till they vanished out of sight. Judy sat back in her chair and closed her eyes for moment.

'What will you have to drink?' asked Alex.

'Oh, just soda water, thanks.'

A drinks waiter dressed in striped convict garb came and took their orders, and was soon followed by a strapping wench in a mob-cap and low-cut Georgian dress, who offered them a basket of hot home-made damper, and menus printed in the form of eighteenth-century newspapers.

'Right,' said Alex, as the waitress departed. 'First we'll eat, and then we'll talk.'

'I'm not really very hungry,' said Judy dispiritedly.

'Now look,' warned Alex, looking severely at her over the top of his newspaper, 'I don't mind your being small and slender, but I certainly don't want you getting anorexic. Now, either you choose something out of there, or I'll order for you.'

'And force-feed me when it arrives?' asked Judy with a wry grin.

'Right,' agreed Alex.

When their orders had been taken, he lounged back in his chair and tore off a large hunk of damper.

'Beautiful day, isn't it?' he said, smiling.

His earlier ill temper seemed to have vanished completely, which only made Judy feel worse. How could he sit there so calmly and cheerfully, when at any moment he was going to tell her that their marriage was over? She looked hungrily at his lean, tanned body, her gaze travelling down over his dark hair and brown eyes, his even white teeth, those powerful shoulders and the tanned arms that had held her so fiercely only last night. Oh, Alex, I love you so, she thought wistfully, and the lump in her throat threatened to rise and choke her. But somehow the thought gave her strength. It wasn't Alex's fault that things hadn't worked out. He had acted generously in marrying her, and it was up to her to be equally generous now.

'Alex?' she said in a small voice.

'Yes?'

'I know you wanted to wait till after dinner to discuss all this, but there's just one thing I want to say now. I'd like you to know that I won't make any difficulties about the divorce, and I'll never try to stop you having access to Robin, or anything like that.'

'Divorce?' exclaimed Alex. He was sitting bolt upright in his chair now, staring at her aghast. 'Access? Judy, what on earth are you talking about?'

His astonishment was too overpowering to be false. The suspicion that she had misunderstood him flitted across her mind, and was instantly followed by a look of relief and embarrassment.

'B—but, Alex, I thought—well, you said . . . . Oh, heavens! This is so——'

She was saved by the arrival of the waitress with two large prawn cocktails. By the time the girl had fussed around serving them, and gathering up the empty damper basket, Judy had regained a little of her composure, but a look of unholy amusement was spreading over Alex's face.

'All right,' he said, grinning as the waitress disappeared into the recesses of the building, 'would you mind just telling me what I said or did that made you so convinced I wanted a divorce?'

'Oh, Alex!' wailed Judy. 'Don't laugh at me like that! It's your own stupid fault. It was what you said this morning.'

'What I said this morning?' asked Alex in a mystified voice. 'What did I say this morning? Surely you're not threatening to divorce me because I shouted at old Banana Man?'

'No, of course not,' said Judy impatiently. 'It's nothing to do with Robin. When I burnt the breakfast, you said, "We just can't go on like this—it's not working," and then in

Theatre this afternoon you said the same sort of thing. I forget the exact words, but it was something about how you thought you were doing the right thing, but it wasn't working out.'

Alex put down his fork, wiped his mouth, sat back in his seat and roared with laughter.

'I don't see what's so funny,' said Judy coldly.

'Oh, Judy!' he uttered between gasps. 'I wasn't talking about our marriage—for heaven's sake, we've only been married a couple of months! I was talking about the house.'

It was Judy's turn to be mystified. 'The house?' she echoed.

'Yes, you know. That oversized pile of bricks and mortar that is driving you slowly crackers. I thought I was doing the right thing by moving you in there, but it's just not working out, is it? Look, why don't we both have a drink, finish our prawn cocktails, and then discuss this thing calmly before the restaurant staff decide they've got a couple of loonies out here?'

Still only half convinced, Judy picked up her glass, but before it even reached her lips she began to see the funny side of the whole affair. The corners of her mouth twitched, she caught Alex's eye, and in a moment the pair of them were chuckling helplessly. Each time one of them seemed about to recover, a fresh spasm would overtake the other one, setting them both off again.

'Enjoying your dinner, are you?' asked the waitress, raising her eyebrows.

'Yes, it's excellent,' choked Alex, vainly trying to sober up as she bustled out of the courtyard with the remains of the prawn cocktail.

But in the end their laughter did die down, and they were able to confront each other. Alex looked at Judy, and thought how attractive she was with her cheeks flushed and her eyes sparkling with amusement. 'You know what?' he said. 'I told myself in Theatre today that I was really going to get to know you. And I think I'm beginning to do it.'

'Did you?' asked Judy, going even pinker with pleasure. 'I'm glad.'

The rest of the meal seemed to slip by in a twinkling. All the constraint had vanished from Judy's manner, and she talked animatedly about medicine and folk music, about Robin's infancy and her own childhood on the northwest coast. Some of her anecdotes were surprisingly witty, and Alex found himself capping them with outrageous and highly suspect stories of things which had—supposedly— happened to him in Canada. It was fun, and, when the waitress came to present the bill, they were both surprised to look up and find that the sky overhead had changed from forget-me-not blue to an apple-green twilight.

'How about a walk?' asked Alex, reluctant to abandon this new-found intimacy.

'That would be lovely,' agreed Judy.

They went up Kelly's Steps, picking their way carefully on the worn sandstone where whalers and shipwrights had trodden a century before. When they emerged in Battery Point, there was just enough light left for them to see Georgian cottages overgrown with jasmine and honeysuckle jumbled up against Victorian terraces and modern brick bungalows. A cat darted underneath the wheels of a parked car at their approach, and an old lady hosing her garden called a good evening to them.

'I love Battery Point,' said Judy. 'It's just like a little village, and yet it's only a hop, skip and a jump from the city centre.'

'Which way do you want to go?' asked Alex.

Judy wrinkled her nose thoughtfully. 'Round to the boatyards,' she replied. 'There'll be a full moon tonight, and it always looks wonderful over the water.'

It did look wonderful. The moon had scarcely risen over the top of the three bare hills across the river, but already its radiance was spilt across miles of shimmering dark water. As they turned into the park by the boatyard, the plaintive cry of plovers rose into the air and vanished above their heads.

'Poor things!' exclaimed Judy. 'It's really their territory, after all.'

'And yours, I suspect,' said Alex. 'I'm beginning to think it was a grave mistake to take you away from all this. You're not really happy where we're living at the moment, are you?'

'No-o,' admitted Judy guardedly. 'Still, I don't want to seem ungrateful. It's a lovely house, and I think Yuri was an absolute sweetie to buy it for us. It's just that it's so much work to keep it going, and Robin did love living here. But, after all, we couldn't have stayed in that tiny flat at Kate's place much longer. And you have to expect to adapt to a few new things when you get married.'

'You certainly do,' said Alex ruefully. 'And I suppose I deserve nought out of ten on that score. I really owe you an apology, Judy.'

'An apology?' said Judy, startled. 'What for?'

'Mmm,' said Alex thoughtfully. 'Arrogance, insensitivity, sheer, unmitigated stupidity. Will that do for a start?'

'What are you talking about?' asked Judy, half laughing.

Alex took her hand and drew her against him, then looked down into her wistful face, his gaze resting affectionately on her sparkling eyes and pointed chin. 'Come and sit on the bench,' he suggested. 'It's a long confession, so I might as well be comfortable while I make it. I'm talking about the way you've been running yourself into the ground, and I didn't even notice it until today. It's unforgivable of me, I know, but maybe that's just what men are like. Still, I should have known better. After all, I went through it all myself, and I know what a hard grind it is being an intern. What's more,

I wasn't trying to cope with a big house and raise a kid at the same time. The trouble is, you were so damned efficient running around doing your Superwoman act that I just didn't notice how hard it all was for you.'

'That's OK,' said Judy gruffly.

'Anyway, the point is that we've got to do something to make life a bit easier for you. The only question is, what?'

'I suppose I could try another housekeeper,' suggested Judy reluctantly.

'I've got a better idea,' said Alex. 'We'll get rid of the house and find something smaller.'

'What?' demanded Judy.

'Don't sound so amazed. It's perfectly reasonable, when you think about it.'

'But Yuri's only just bought it. He'd be so hurt. And it really is a lovely place.'

'Well, we don't have to sell it,' said Alex. 'We could let it out. Let's see. You finish your internship next month, and then you've got another year at St Thomas's as a resident, right?'

'Yes.'

'Well, then, we'll let it out for a year or so, and find ourselves a nice little place here in Battery Point instead. They you'll be close to the hospital and Robin will be near the babysitter. And perhaps you could get someone in just for a couple of hours a day to do cleaning. You wouldn't mind that, would you?'

Judy thought it over.

'No, I wouldn't,' she agreed. 'I just didn't like having somebody living in, being underfoot all the time.'

'Good,' said Alex buoyantly. 'A daily cleaner, then. That suits me, because I may be feeling guilty, but I don't feel guilty enough to do the vacuuming and washing up.'

Judy grinned and leant her head spontaneously against him. 'Oh, Alex, you are nice!' she said. 'Are you sure you don't mind about the house?'

'No, of course not,' he replied. 'Anyway, we can always move back there later on, when we're ready to have more children.'

'Ch-children?'

'Yes. Don't you want more?'

'Yes, I do. But I thought . . . Well, that is . . . We never really discussed it.'

'There are a lot of things we never discussed,' said Alex. 'But we'll get round to them. After all, we've got our whole lives left to sort it all out. All the time in the world to find out about each other.'

He pulled her into his arms then, and kissed her, a long, tender kiss that left her aching with desire. Then his warm fingers came up and played with the silky fragrance of her hair.

'Oh, Judy!' he said, drawing her close against him. 'Judy, Judy, Judy. I'm beginning to think marrying you was the best thing I've ever done.'

When Judy came to work the next day she positively glowed with happiness and vitality. David Carstairs encountered her on a ward round and could hardly believe his eyes.

'Well, you look a lot better than you did yesterday!' he said. 'You really had a good night's sleep, did you?'

Judy swallowed a smile.

'Or didn't, as the case may be,' said David suggestively. 'Ah, well, some of us have our nights of passion and others only dream about it. And, while we're on the subject of dreams, get a load of this. You know that nurse I was telling you about yesterday? She's on Paediatrics again. Just take a look. Isn't she a stunner?'

As he spoke, he was flinging open the door to the ward. Judy followed him in, laughing. But the laughter died on her lips. There at the desk, with her blonde hair twisted into a coil and her long legs crossed, sat Stephanie Hargreaves.

CHAPTER SIX

'IT MUST have given you quite a shock to see her there,' said Kate sympathetically. She walked carefully across her living-room, balancing a tray with two mugs, kicked a plastic duck out of the way and sat down on the couch.

'You're not kidding,' agreed Judy. 'It was the biggest jolt I've had since I discovered I was pregnant with Robin. But what's she here for? That's what I'd like to know.'

'You did say she was using her maiden name, didn't you?'

'That's right. "Nurse S. Hargreaves", it said on her badge.'

'Then I suppose that means she's split up from her husband,' murmured Kate thoughtfully.

'Well, in that case,' said Judy slowly, 'she might have come back here because of Alex. Oh, Kate, do you think she has?'

Kate pursed her lips and then shook her head. 'I doubt it, Judy,' she said at last. 'After all, she was the one who threw him over, not vice versa. And anyway, even if she has, she's just out of luck, isn't she? He's married to you now, and that's that.'

'I know,' said Judy unhappily, twining her fingers round her mug and sipping slowly. 'But he was really crazy about her, you know. He still carries a picture of her in his wallet. I found it one day when I was looking for some change to buy bread.'

'I'd murder him for that,' said Kate indignantly.

'Oh, it's not that simple,' protested Judy. 'He really only married me in the first place because of Robin, so I can't go round playing the jealous wife and throwing scenes all the time. Anyway, it's only a photo.'

'That's true,' agreed Kate comfortingly. 'Besides, from what you were saying, you really seem to be getting along well now. He must really care about you, if he's going to give up the big house just so you can be close to work.'

'I know,' said Judy, smiling at the thought. 'But that's the whole problem. I don't want Stephanie round ruining things just when we've started to get to know each other. Oh, help! I wish I knew what her plans were.'

'Well, perhaps Richard can tell you something.'

'Richard?' asked Judy blankly.

'Yes, dodo! Richard Pryor. You know, Richard, the anaesthetist, Alex's friend, the best man at your wedding?'

'Oh, that Richard,' said Judy vaguely, and then added with sudden interest, 'Are you still seeing him?'

'That's right. We've been getting along like a house on fire ever since your wedding. In fact, I really ought to thank you for bringing us together. I knew Richard slightly before, but I don't think he would ever have invited me out if we hadn't been thrown together so much.'

'Serious, is it?' asked Judy.

Kate blushed and smiled. 'Well, it's really too soon to tell,' she confessed, 'but I'm hoping. Anyway, the point is that Richard's always really well up on all the hospital gossip. If anyone knows what Stephanie's plans are, he will.'

'When are you seeing him again?' asked Judy curiously.

'He's supposed to be coming round this morning on his way to work. He borrowed my electric extension cord and he's going to drop it off.'

Just at that moment the doorbell rang, and Kate flew to the front door. A moment later she came back with Richard in tow, carrying a large orange coil on his arm. Judy looked at them, thinking what a good-looking couple they were—both tall and suntanned, but Richard as blond as Kate was dark.

'Got time for a cup of coffee?' asked Kate.

'Yes, please,' agreed Richard. 'Hello, Judy. How are things?'

'Not bad, thanks,' said Judy guardedly.

He sat down opposite her, and they launched into an easy flow of banter and hospital gossip. But Judy shied away from the one piece of gossip that really interested her. Kate, when she came back with the coffee, had no such scruples.

'Richard,' she said bluntly, sitting down beside him, 'do you have any idea why Stephanie Hargreaves is back in Hobart?'

'Yes, I do,' said Richard, taking a long gulp of coffee. 'Rumour has it that her husband lost a lot of money in the stock-market crash, and the marriage is over. Mind you, it was on the rocks already. They'd both been going around with other people and that sort of thing. But it took a severe trauma to the hip-pocket nerve to finish it off entirely.'

'Judy's worried that Stephanie might be back here to pursue Alex. You don't think it's true, do you?'

'I wouldn't put it past her,' said Richard bluntly. 'After all, when it comes to gold-digging, old Stephanie doesn't just go in with her long scarlet fingernails, she uses a front-end loader. As far as I know, the Shaw fortune is still looking pretty healthy, and Stephanie always had a special feeling for Alex. In so far as Stephanie ever had any feelings, that is.'

'Wow!' said Kate. 'You really don't like her, do you?'

'No,' said Richard.

'But all that stuff with Alex is in the past, surely?' persisted Kate. 'After all, he's married now.'

'Stephanie wouldn't let a little thing like that stop her,' said Richard bitterly. 'And, if you take my advice, Judy, you'll keep an eye on her. I don't think it's any coincidence that she's been posted to Paediatrics. So, if she's after Alex, she'll probably make a move pretty soon before she gets transferred somewhere else. But you just give her the elbow, if she does.

Let her know you won't stand for it.'

'How can I?' asked Judy miserably. 'I can't stand guard over him all the time. And, anyway, if Alex really loves her, perhaps I don't have any real right to interfere. After all, she was the one he really wanted to marry.'

Richard made a rude noise. 'Like hell you don't have any right to interfere,' he said. 'You're his wife, aren't you? And a damned sight better one than Stephanie would ever had made him. Besides, apart from your rights, Alex is my friend and I don't want to see him trapped by that designing little——'

'Richard!' said Kate.

'All right, I wasn't going to say it, but it's what I think of her, just the same. Anyway, thanks for the coffee. Can I give you a lift to the hospital, Judy?'

'Thanks, Richard. I'll just say goodbye to Robin and then I'll be ready.'

Judy took Richard's advice about keeping an eye on Stephanie, and she soon realised that the other girl was making a determined effort to attract Alex's attention. Twice Stephanie 'just happened' to bump into them as Alex was picking Judy up from work, and, on another occasion when Judy answered the phone at home, there was silence at the other end, followed by a click as the receiver was hung up. So, when Alex was late collecting her from work one evening, Judy decided to go and look for him. It was nothing unusual for one or the other of them to be delayed, but this time some instinct led her up to the paediatrics ward.

Sure enough, the moment she entered the room she saw them together. It was only three weeks till Christmas, and Stephanie was up on a ladder decorating the Christmas tree which had been donated to the children's ward by the local Lions Club. Down on the floor, Alex stood with a piece of tinsel draped over one arm and a glass bauble in the other hand. As Judy watched, he reached up and offered the ornament to Stephanie. Stephanie glanced back at him, stretched out her hand, then gave a little shriek and fell off the ladder, straight into Alex's arms.

Just at that moment one of the children created a diversion. Five-year-old Sarah Blacklow, who was suffering from gastroenteritis, suddenly clutched her hands across her tummy, moaned weakly and was sick all over her bed. Judy had never been so grateful in her life.

'Excuse me, Nurse Hargreaves,' she said sweetly. 'One of the children has just vomited here. Could you come over and clean her up, please? Oh, and Alex, we'd better dash off now or we'll never get through all our Christmas shopping.'

Later on, as they drove home with a car full of brightly wrapped parcels, Alex stole a speculative glance at Judy. She had not actually said anything about Stephanie, but he had seen the stormy look on her face when she'd entered the ward and found them together. He was surprised and oddly flattered to realise that she was jealous of Stephanie, but at the same time it made him feel obscurely guilty. Not that Judy could reasonably blame him for catching the girl as she fell off the ladder. But he was shrewd enough to guess that Stephanie had done it on purpose, and he was also very confused about his own feelings. Having Stephanie literally drop into his arms had shaken him, and holding her warm curves and smelling her fragrant hair had brought back memories that were probably better forgotten. He stole another glance at Judy and sighed. Poor old Jude. She was reliable and amusing, and one of these days she was going to turn into a really first-class doctor, but when it came to looks she simply couldn't hold a candle to Stephanie. Still, it was Judy he had married, and for everybody's sake he would just have to put Stephanie right out of his mind.

Alex was doing a reasonably good job at this, until a fortnight before Christmas, when trouble blew up. He had found a small house to rent in Battery Point close to Kate's place, and he and Judy had decided to have a combined house-warming and pre-Christmas barbecue. All their closest friends from the hospital had been invited, the weather was sizzling with heat, and it promised to be a tremendous bash. Judy had had one nasty moment when she was making up the guest list with Kate, but it had soon passed.

'David Carstairs and partner,' Judy had said. 'Hmm. He couldn't possibly bring Stephanie, could he?'

'What? Stephanie Hargreaves go out with a penniless intern? She'd crawl a mile over broken glass before she'd do that. No. Go ahead and invite him, Judy.'

So Judy had. But when she opened the door to the first guests, she saw that her worst fears had come true. There stood David, beaming proudly, with Stephanie in a low-cut white jumpsuit that showed off her tan, tossing back her ash-blonde hair and smiling radiantly.

The party went with such a swing that Judy had no time to notice what Stephanie was doing for the first couple of hours. She was kept too busy circulating among the guests, changing records, barbecuing steak and tossing salad. But at about three o'clock, when the uproar had subsided a little and most of the guests were sprawled peacefully in deckchairs under the trees, she saw David waving to her over the heads of a cluster of surgeons and anaesthetists who were arguing the rival merits of nitrous oxide and halothane. She squirmed through the crowd to meet him.

'Hello, David. How's it going?'

'Not so good,' said David ruefully. 'The shish kebab was terrific, but Stephanie seems to have run out on me. Still, I can always have another beer, can't I? Oh, no, don't tell me the old amber fluid's run out too.'

He stood staring with such comic dismay at the thin trickle of liquid in the bottom of his glass that Judy took pity on him. 'I'll get you another bottle,' she offered. 'I have to go inside anyway.'

Her sandals had been chafing her for the last half-hour, and when she reached the kitchen she kicked them off and wiggled her toes gratefully. An inspection of the fridge revealed that all the beer had disappeared, and she decided to try the cellar. Although the house was only a small Georgian cottage, the Georgians had evidently had their priorities right, for it had a neat little wine cellar tucked away below ground level. Judy opened the tiny door and padded softly downwards, her bare feet making no sound on the stone steps. But, as she turned the final corner at the bottom, she came upon a sight which took her breath away. In the opposite corner next to the wine racks stood Alex and Stephanie, locked in a passionate embrace. For a moment Judy stood frozen, part of her brain registering numbly how Stephanie's arms were twined around Alex's neck and how her lips were parted against his. Then, blinded by tears, she turned and fled back up the stairs.

The rest of the afternoon was a nightmare to Judy, something she had to stumble through as best she could. When she and Alex stood side by side at the gate, farewelling their guests, she was subdued and pale, and she saw him glance at her uneasily. And later on, when they went upstairs to bed in their little attic room, she pleaded a headache and turned her back on him, only to lie awake for hours staring miserably into the darkness. She wondered whether Alex would mention the incident himself, confess, explain, say something—she could not imagine what—which would make her feel better. But he said nothing. And before long his breathing grew quiet and regular, so that she knew he was asleep. That seemed like the worst treachery of all—the fact that he could sleep as if nothing had happened. As if kissing Stephanie did not worry him in the least.

In fact, Judy was wrong. Kissing Stephanie worried Alex a great deal. What had happened had taken him completely by surprise, for Stephanie had gone into raptures over the little cottage and begged for a guided tour. However, once they had been alone in the cellar, she had suddenly twined her arms around his neck and drawn his head down to hers. For a moment of madness, he had responded eagerly, kissing her with passionate fervour. It was bad luck that Judy had chosen that precise moment to come down the stairs, and even worse luck that she had immediately fled again. For, a moment later, Alex had pushed Stephanie roughly away and paced swiftly across the room, running his fingers through his hair.

'For heaven's sake, Stephanie!' he had grated. 'We just can't do this any more. I'm a married man now!'

Stephanie's only response had been a little silvery laugh. And as she had stood there, her hair tumbling over her shoulders and her blue eyes mocking, he had wanted her. Wanted her desperately, insanely. He had stifled a groan. That was the trouble. He still wanted her.

For a couple of days Alex and Judy went around on edge. Judy was hurt beyond measure by what she had seen, and kept wondering gloomily whether she ought to offer Alex a divorce. Alex, on the other hand, was completely unaware that Judy had seen anything at all, and felt vaguely ill-used. After all, he had moved house to please her, and he had—in the end—resisted Stephanie's blandishments, so he felt Judy had no right to go moping around like a wet week. Didn't she appreciate all that he had done for her? Obviously not.

But in the end, when they did quarrel, it was not about the things that were really distressing them. Or, at least, not at first.

Alex came home tired and irritable at eleven o'clock one

night, after an emergency bowel-obstruction operation, to find Judy sitting up watching an old movie on TV. It was a classic 'weepie' from the 1950s, and Judy was equipped with a box of tissues and a bowl of peanuts to see her through it. She was blowing her nose energetically as he came into the living-room, and, when he walked unthinkingly in front of the television set, she gestured crossly to him to move. Usually, when he came home, she would kiss him on the cheek, ask him about his day, offer him something to drink. Without even realising it, he had come to look forward to these little attentions, and he felt hurt now that they were missing. Grumpily he strode into the kitchen and made himself a cup of hot chocolate, which he brought back out with him. Then he sat on the couch beside her.

'Judy——' he began.

'Oh, shush, Alex,' she pleaded. 'Not now.'

He sat in silence for a couple of minutes, his eyes flickering backwards and forwards from the television to his wife. It was hard to believe she could be so mesmerised by that stuff. On the screen, a woman with her hair in two crimped bunches was sitting woefully at a table staring at a calendar. As she sat, the leaves fell rapidly off the calendar —what a brilliant device for suggesting the passage of time! thought Alex ironically—and her face grew steadily more wretched, while in the background an asthmatic record player gave a garbled rendition of Vera Lynn singing 'We'll Meet Again'.

'What's going on?' asked Alex, determined to get Judy's attention.

She shot him a suspicious glance, and then replied in a stage whisper. 'Her husband has left her for another woman, and it's almost their fifth wedding anniversary. When they first got married, he said he'd give her one more red carnation on each anniversary, and it's nearly midnight now and he hasn't come.

Oh, wait a minute. Look!'

The camera cut away from the calendar to a moonlit railway station. In the background sirens wailed and there was the loud, rushing noise of an oncoming train. Then a man with a suitcase and a tall, blonde girl moved forward towards the edge of the platform. But, as they did so, a woman carrying a wooden tray approached them. The man put out his hand to wave her away, and then saw what she was selling. The tray was full of red carnations. He gave a start, and stood for a moment, irresolute. Then the camera drew away so that the people grew very tiny, like figures seen through the wrong end of a telescope. The man fumbling in his pocket for coins, the girl clinging to his arm and being shaken off, the train pulling slowly away from the station without them. Judy gave a little, gulping sob and dabbed at her eyes with a tissue as the scene changed again. Back to the house where the wife sat weeping and watching the clock. Then, just before the stroke of midnight, a key turned in the door and her husband came hesitantly in, clutching a bunch of carnations. Predictably, he swept her into his arms, the carnations were tossed on to the hall table, and it all ended happily ever after.

'I don't know how you can watch that rubbish,' said Alex, striding over to the television set and switching it off the moment the final embrace was ended.

'It's not rubbish,' said Judy indignantly, striding over and switching it back on. 'And anyway, I want to see who was playing the flower seller.'

The credits continued to roll up, the music went on playing, and the carnations sat in the centre of the screen with a wedding photo suggestively beside them. Alex waited with exaggerated patience until the last frame disappeared and Judy's curiosity was satisfied, then returned to the attack.

'It's such trash,' he complained. 'I mean, London in the middle of the Blitz and that pair are running off together at midnight? Why midnight, for heaven's sake? And a woman just happens to be out on the platform selling flowers at that hour. Flowers! Gas masks would be more like it!'

'Oh, don't be so hateful!' said Judy. 'You didn't have to watch it if you didn't want to. So why does it bother you so much?'

'Well,' said Alex weakly, 'I just don't like to see you wasting your time on that sort of nonsense. After all, real people don't behave like that.'

'No, of course not,' flashed Judy. 'Real people don't leave their wives and get involved with other women, do they?'

There was a deadly silence. Across the room their eyes met and locked, and Alex felt the hairs on the back of his neck rise up and prickle.

'What are you talking about?' he asked softly.

'I'm talking about the film,' said Judy evenly.

'Oh, no, you're not,' said Alex. 'Are you?'

'No, I'm not,' agreed Judy at last. 'I'm talking about you kissing Stephanie down in the cellar last week.'

Alex groaned. 'How did you know about that?' he asked.

'I saw it happen. And, from where I was standing, it looked real enough.'

'What can I say?' said Alex, spreading his hands out and slumping into a chair. 'I'm sorry, Judy. I'm really sorry. It should never have happened.'

'No,' agreed Judy in a tight voice. 'But it did happen.'

'Look, I don't expect you to understand, but it all took me completely by surprise. One minute I was there showing Stephanie the wine racks, and the next moment she was all over me. But it was only a kiss. Nothing else has happened between us.'

'Not yet, perhaps,' said Judy bitterly. 'But give her time.'

'No!' urged Alex. 'Judy, please, you've got to believe me. That wasn't what I intended when I married you. Nothing like this will ever happen again. I swear it.'

'Oh, Alex,' said Judy in a voice that was softer, but still troubled. 'I suppose you mean that now, but how can you be so sure? After all, you're still in love with Stephanie, aren't you?'

Alex paused. A hot denial sprang to his lips, but honesty held it back. He thought of Stephanie's limpid, violet-blue eyes, the peachlike texture of her skin, the way her body curved into his when he touched her. Then he remembered how she had left him nearly five years before. How she had just run out on him and married somebody else, and pain flooded through him.

'I don't know,' he said honestly. 'But that's neither here nor there. What's love, anyway? It's just a word, and it doesn't mean very much. I'm married to you, and that's what really counts.'

'And what's marriage?' asked Judy fiercely. 'Isn't that just a word too? One that doesn't mean very much?'

'No!' said Alex hotly. 'Look, I told you when I first proposed to you that I thought it was our duty to get married for Robin's sake. And I stand by that.'

'Duty!' said Judy, spitting out the word as if it were something rather cold and nasty. 'Well, if that's all we're ever going to have between us, I think we ought to give up right now.'

'You mean get a divorce?' asked Alex incredulously.

'Yes,' said Judy. 'I mean get a divorce.'

She could scarcely believe the pain that overwhelmed her when she said these words. It couldn't be true, it couldn't be her, standing here giving Alex the chance to leave her — in fact, almost begging him to go. But something relentless drove her on. She gasped for breath and then grew calmer.

'But why?' demanded Alex.

'Because duty isn't enough for me,' said Judy in a rush.

'Because I don't want to be married to someone who is only staying with me for my son's sake. If we can't have something more than that between us, just the two of us, then I'd rather have a clean break right now.'

'I know what it is,' said Alex bitterly. 'It's all that romantic stuff you watch on television. I suppose if I went around buying you carnations and telling you I adored you all the time, you'd be perfectly happy. But that's all so stupid. Why can't you learn to cope with reality?'

'Reality?' said Judy, gulping. 'You know, Alex, I always thought I did pretty well at coping with reality. We get rather a lot of it in our line of work, or hadn't you noticed? I sat with a twelve-year old girl this afternoon who's got an advanced case of acute lymphoblastic leukaemia, and afterwards I tried to tell her mother that she probably won't live more than another three months. I'd say that was coping with reality. But, in any case, why does reality always have to mean the harshest and nastiest side of life? What's unreal about love? Or tenderness? Or saying things that make people feel good about themselves? Yes, since you ask, I could do with a few carnations.'

'Judy, you're just twisting everything I say! Here I am, trying to tell you that I'm not going off with Stephanie; that I don't want a divorce, and all you can do is make me out to be some kind of ogre, just because I won't say nice things to you. Well, there are lots of things I like about you. You're loyal and reliable, and you're good at your job. You're a great mother, you're really pretty sexy and you cook terrific shish kebabs.'

'But you don't love me, do you?' whispered Judy, a tremulous smile flitting across her face as she listened to this odd catalogue of her virtues.

'There you go again!' growled Alex, looking uncannily like Yuri in the middle of one of his rages. 'Love! Love!

What's that got to do with it?'

'Everything!' shouted Judy. 'Everything, you pig-headed, insensitive, arrogant——'

Just at that moment the doorbell rang. They stared at each other in bewilderment.

'I wonder who on earth that is at this hour of the night,' said Alex.

'You'd better go,' said Judy bitterly. 'It's probably Stephanie coming back for another look at the wine racks.'

But it wasn't Stephanie. It was Celeste. She tripped lightly into the room, still managing to look poised and carefree, in spite of the two heavy suitcases she was carrying. Alex strode forward to help her with them.

'*Maman*!' he said, kissing her on the cheek. 'Whatever are you doing here?'

'I had to come over on business, so I thought it would be a good chance to bring your Christmas presents with me and to see Robin.' Her glance travelled sharply between them. 'You've been quarrelling, haven't you?'

'No,' said Judy.

'Yes,' said Alex.

Celeste laughed.

'Oh, lovers' quarrels!' she said. 'How wonderful to be young enough for lovers' quarrels! Of course, at my age one is more interested in a large gin and tonic . . .'

She looked hopefully at Alex, and he raised his eyebrows and went into the kitchen.

'Drink, Judy?' he called back.

'A small gin and tonic, please.'

When Alex returned with the drinks, Judy was composed enough to smile at him as if nothing had happened. All the same, she had the uneasy feeling that Celeste's eyes were boring right through her and seeing everything.

'Why didn't you phone and tell us you were coming?'

asked Alex.

'I tried,' said Celeste. 'Several times. But the phone was always engaged.'

They sat chatting for a few minutes, but the conversation centred mostly on the family business. Before long, Judy excused herself and went to bed, thankful to escape Celeste's occasional probing glances. The next morning she was not so lucky. When she came downstairs at six o'clock, she found her mother-in-law already in the kitchen, brewing coffee.

'I hope you don't mind, *chérie*,' she apologised. 'But I always wake early, and my coffee I simply must have.'

'That's all right,' said Judy. 'I'm the same really.'

'Then come and have a cup with me, and tell me what's going on with you and Alex. Is it serious, this quarrel?'

Judy sighed and slumped into a chair.

'Yes,' she admitted.

'May one ask what it is about?'

'It's about Stephanie Hargreaves. She's come back and she won't leave Alex alone. She's been making nuisance calls on the phone.'

'Oh, my dear!' said Celeste, parting her soothingly on the hand. 'You just tell me all about it and we'll see what we can work out.'

Surprisingly Judy, who would not have dreamt of confiding in her own mother, found herself pouring out the whole story to Alex's. Celeste was full of sympathy, clicking her tongue and exclaiming over Stephanie's impertinence. When Judy finally came to a halt, the older woman clasped her hands together and then set her elbows squarely on the table, as if she were getting ready to chair a meeting.

'*Eh, bien!*' she said. 'If she wants war, this Stephanie, we will give her war. You must fight back, Judy! Don't just give in and let her take your husband without a struggle.'

'But she's the one Alex really loves,' said Judy

despairingly.

'*Ma foi*' said Celeste. 'I begin to think you are as big a fool as my son. Let me tell you, my dear, that Alex is already far more attached to you than he realises himself. He telephones me two or three times a week. You know that, don't you? And always it is, "Judy is doing this, Judy is doing that, Judy cooks wonderful terrines, Judy and I went bushwalking, Judy, Judy, Judy . . ." I tell you, if he were ever unfortunate enough to divorce you and marry her, it would not take him long to see what a bad bargain he had made.'

A reluctant smile had begun to spread over Judy's face. 'But what can I do?' she demanded.

'To begin with, you must spend some time completely alone with him. Somewhere romantic, for preference. Now, are you free this weekend, both of you? Good. Then you must book a room in a motel somewhere really special and go away together.'

'But Robin——' began Judy.

Celeste dismissed this with a wave of her hand.

'What could be simpler? I will stay on here for a few days and mind him. That is what grandmothers are for, *n'est-ce pas*?'

'Oh, Celeste!' said Judy, squeezing her hand spontaneously. 'You are—what's the word?—*merveilleuse*!'

Later the same morning, Judy slipped into the clinical library for a quick word with Kate. She was disappointed to find the reference desk empty, and was just turning to leave when Kate appeared at her elbow.

'Oh, there you are!' said Judy. 'I thought you were out.'

'I had to go into the other room to receive a fax,' said Kate. 'By the way, nobody else came in, did they? It's just that I've got some urgent stuff waiting here for Prof Castle and I don't want to miss him.'

'I don't think so,' said Judy, glancing around. 'The place seems empty.'

'Well, what can I do for you, then?' asked Kate. 'Is this business or pleasure?'

'Pleasure, I suppose you'd call it,' said Judy. 'I just came in to ask you whether you'd mind if we don't come in for drinks tomorrow evening.'

'No, of course not,' said Kate, grinning. 'Got a better invitation, have you?'

'Oh, Kate, don't be ridiculous! No. It's just that Alex's mother, Celeste, has come down unexpectedly and she thinks Alex and I should have a weekend away while she babysits.'

'Now that's what I call the right kind of mother-in-law!' said Kate admiringly. 'Where are you going to?'

'We haven't really decided yet,' said Judy. 'I'd like to go bushwalking, but I don't want to camp out. What I'd really like is wilderness during the day and luxury at night. But it's rather a difficult combination to come by!'

'Why don't you try that new wilderness lodge down near Hastings? Richard was telling me about it. Apparently it's just opened, and the food and accommodation are terrific. Turner's Wilderness Lodge, it's called. I've got a pamphlet somewhere here with the details. Yes, here it is.'

'Thanks,' said Judy. 'All right. We'll give it a try.'

She took out a notepad and scribbled down the details.

'You might see Richard down that way, actually,' said Kate. 'He's going on a caving excursion this weekend with the Caving Club. But don't worry. They're staying in the old walkers' huts, so they won't be underfoot spoiling your romantic weekend at the lodge.'

'Caving,' said Judy thoughtfully. 'Alex used to go caving years ago. Celeste showed me some photos of him once, all dressed up like a miner. But it doesn't appeal to me.'

'Me neither,' said Kate, repressing a shudder. 'Richard

wanted me to come too, but I'm working this Saturday, which is a good excuse. Just as well, really. Bats!'

'Darkness, tunnels in the rock, creepy crawlies!' agreed Judy. 'Ugh! No, thanks.'

There was a sudden sharp ding! from the room next door.

'Oh, that's the fax machine again,' said Kate. 'I'll have to go. Well, have a good time.'

'Thanks. I must fly too—I'm on my coffee-break. See you on Monday.'

A moment later there was a stealthy movement behind the book stacks. A white-clad figure came out, looking swiftly around to make sure that Kate and Judy had both gone. Then Stephanie Hargreaves sauntered casually across to Kate's desk, picked up the pamphlet about Turner's Wilderness Lodge, and, smiling secretively, walked out of the library.

CHAPTER SEVEN

THE phone shrilled insistently. Judy, staggering in from the carport with two enormous bags of groceries, half expected it to be Stephanie. She kicked the kitchen door shut, dropped the groceries and snatched up the receiver, mentally preparing herself to slam it down again. But it was Alex.

'Judy? Is Robin around? No? Good. Listen, was it tonight we were meant to go shopping for his Christmas presents?'

'Yes,' said Judy. 'Celeste's taken him to the pantomime specially to get him out of the way while we smuggle the stuff in. Don't say you've got emergency surgery again?'

'It's not quite that bad,' Alex reassured her. 'But I will be held up. You remember that kid Michael Burrows who had the kidney tumour three months back?'

'Yes,' said Judy, her heart in her mouth.

'His GP has just rung me. Apparently Michael's there with him, and he's not too well. His mother's worried sick about him, so as a special favour I've told her to bring him round to my rooms right now and I'll run a couple of tests. If I send them to the path lab first thing in the morning, we should have some results by tomorrow afternoon. It might save her worrying all weekend. But I can't get home at six to pick you up. Can you meet me in town instead? Some of the stores have late-night shopping, so we can still get the presents.'

'I'll be there in ten minutes,' Judy promised.

When she arrived at Alex's rooms, Judy found that the receptionist had already locked up and left, so she had to use her own key to let herself into the building. The dimness of the waiting-room was overpowering after the bright sunshine outside, and for a moment Judy did not see the figure huddled next to the unlit Christmas tree. Then a muffled sob caught her attention.

'Mrs Burrows!' she said. 'Whatever's the matter? Do you remember me? I'm Dr Shaw. I used to be Dr Lacey.'

'Oh, yes,' replied Mrs Burrows in a stifled voice. 'You were so kind to Michael, visiting him in Melbourne and everything. I'm sorry to put you and Mr Shaw out like this, seeing him after hours, especially at Christmas time, but I just don't know what to do.'

'I'll tell you what,' said Judy, 'why don't you have a nice cup of coffee and tell me all about it? Where's Michael, by the way?'

'In with Mr Shaw,' said Mrs Burrows, twisting her handkerchief between her fingers.

There was an urn in the corner, which Alex kept for patients to make coffee, and Judy switched this on and then, on impulse, turned on the Christmas-tree lights as well. A soft multicoloured glow filled the room.

'There, that's better!' said Judy with satisfaction. 'Now, won't you tell me what's upsetting you?'

'It's Michael,' said Mrs Burrows hesitantly. 'He doesn't seem at all well, and I'm just so worried and confused about everything.'

'Well, it was a pretty serious operation,' said Judy soothingly. 'You must expect it to take time for him to get back to normal.'

She did not voice her own fear that the tumour might have regenerated. Time enough to worry about that when the results of Alex's tests were in.

'Yes, but it's more than just the operation,' said Mrs Burrows in a sudden confidential burst. She rose to her feet and paced around the room. 'Everything just seems to be getting on top of us. Family problems as well as Michael's health. You see, Michael just doesn't get along with my husband at all . . .'

She saw Judy's puzzled frown and came to a halt.

'Adrian isn't his real father,' she said bleakly. 'Only his stepfather. You see, I was a single mother, and for years there were only the two of us. We were so close; we did everything together. And then I met Adrian. I thought I was doing the right thing by marrying again, giving Michael a father, and I was so lonely. But now I'm beginning to think I made a terrible mistake!'

Her voice rose on a sob, and she flung herself down in a chair and covered her face with her hands. For one fleeting moment Judy had some awful misgivings about the ethics of the situation she was in, but sturdily she dismissed them. After all, even if none of the Burrows family was her patient, she could hardly just walk out when the poor woman was so upset. The urn in the corner let out a welcome bubbling sound, and she hurried over to turn it off.

'How do you like your coffee, Mrs Burrows?' she asked. 'Milk, two sugars? There you are, then.'

The other woman accepted the coffee gratefully and took a long gulp. 'I'm sorry to burden you with all this,' she said guiltily. 'But the strain of it all is making me feel quite ill. And I'm sure it's at the root of some of Michael's problems too. He's a nice kid at heart, you know, but not a bit like the way Adrian wants him to be. Adrian's never had much to do with children, you see, and he wants Michael to be quiet and studious and hard-working. Well, he's certainly quiet now. Sits in his room, won't eat, won't talk—you'd hardly think it was the same child. But his school reports aren't getting any better, and I don't think they ever will. And Adrian just won't get off his back about it.'

'Have you talked to anyone else about this?' asked Judy. 'Mr Shaw or a family counsellor?'

Mrs Burrows shook her head, smiling through her tears.

'I think it's all been building up like Vesuvius waiting to erupt,' she confessed.

'Then would you object if I told Mr Shaw? I can't help feeling that it might have a lot to do with Michael's slow recovery, and he really ought to know. He could put you in touch with an excellent counsellor through the hospital.'

Mrs Burrows hesitated, and then nodded.

'I'll do anything if you think it will help Michael,' she said

'Then I'll discuss it with him this weekend,' Judy promised.

'So, you see,' finished Judy, 'she thinks his emotional problems are slowing his recovery down.'

Alex frowned thoughtfully and rubbed his chin. 'She could be right at that,' he said. 'After all, there was nothing seriously wrong with the test results. The scan didn't show any sign of the tumour regenerating, thank God! And his blood count was a bit low, but nothing really severe. Just the sort of mild anaemia you'd expect after an operation like that. And yet the kid himself looks pathetic—weak, pale, listless. I'll tell you what, I'll have a word to the husband myself, and advise him to ease up on the boy. And I'll also get them referred to a family counsellor. If Mrs Burrows can persuade her husband to go along with it, it might be just what young Michael needs. Now, are you going to loaf around all day drinking juice, or are we going to climb this mountain?'

Judy aimed a lazy kick at him, but he was already up and striding along the track. Stretching luxuriously, she began to collect the cups and papers, and glanced happily around her. It was a glorious day. High up above the canopy of leaves, the sun blazed in a sky that was almost a tropical blue. Judy rose to her feet, adjusting the strap of her pack, and took a deep breath. The air was heavy with the aroma of eucalyptus leaves and the darker, stranger odours of damp rainforest and rotting vegetation. Ahead of her she could see Alex, wending his way along the track that wound in and out between the lacy foliage of manferns.

'Oy!' she shouted. 'How about waiting for the troops, General?'

He came back then, his face alight with laughter, and she felt a little catch in her throat at the sight of him. He was so tall and powerfully built, and yet so graceful, like some animal that belonged out here in the wild. As he reached her, he dropped his pack, took off his hat, and ran his fingers through his hair to cool his hot forehead.

'Whoo! It's going to be a scorcher today,' he said. 'Do you think you're really up to climbing all the way to the waterfall and back? Or would you rather drive down to the pool at Hastings and go for a swim?'

'Well, if you're looking for an excuse to back out . . .' said Judy challengingly.

'Right!' said Alex. 'You've had it, sweetie. That was your last chance. From now on, you're on a forced march under the command of Generalissimo Shaw. Long, hot slogging over rugged terrain, pitiful meals of—of—what's in that lunchbox they gave us from the Lodge?'

'Smoked salmon patties,' said Judy. 'Fillet steak for the barbecue, green salad, French bread, a carton of fresh raspberries.'

'Well, fairly pitiful meals,' said Alex, grinning. 'And at night, just when you think you've escaped the rigours of the Generalissimo's rule, he'll come creeping in beside you on your wretched bedroll and have his wicked way with you.'

'Not in the daytime?' asked Judy in disappointed tones.

'Don't tempt me,' said Alex, coming closer.

In a single fluid movement, he stripped her pack from her shoulders and dropped it on the ground. Then his arms came around her, strong and warm and persuasive. She trembled at the nearness of his body, feeling herself yielding against him as his hands caressed her hair, held the delicate softness of her cheeks, and then travelled lazily, teasingly down over the gentle swell of her breasts.

'Mmm,' she murmured, leaning against him and rubbing her cheek against the coarse fabric of his bushwalking shirt. 'Oh, Alex, that feels so nice . . .'

'It certainly does,' said Alex, sliding his hands in under her clothes and caressing her naked flesh. Then he drew them out again and calmly began to unbutton her blouse.

'Alex!' she protested. 'Someone might see us!'

'Alex!' he mocked. 'Someone might see us! A wallaby or brush-tailed possum. Or, worst of all, a currawong might fly overhead, and then where would we be?'

She fought for breath, her body quivering with pleasure under those expert fingers. 'There might be other bushwalkers,' she whispered. Slowly, reluctantly, he withdrew his hands, touching her on the nose with one fingertip as he did. 'Yes, I suppose there might,' he sighed. Then he stretched himself, adjusted the waistband of his jeans, and looked at her with a gaze that seemed to burn right through her. 'But tonight nothing will save you. And that's a promise.'

Judy smiled secretly and lowered her eyes. They were back to where they had been in New Zealand on their honeymoon, with that mysterious language of looks and smiles. All through the rest of the day, she was conscious of Alex's gaze travelling over her body as she moved, and knew she was assessing him in the same way.

They stopped for lunch at a fast-flowing creek, where they barbecued the steak over a campfire built 'courtesy of boy scout extraordinaire, Alex Shaw' and afterwards they scrambled up over the rocky outcrops to the waterfall above. It was wonderful sitting there, cooled by the flying spray, with nothing to do but look at the panorama spread out below them. The dense grey-green of the rainforest spread out for miles like a huge blanket, bordered on the east by a pale strip of sandy beaches and the deep, intense blue of the Southern Ocean. Turning in the other direction and craning her head, Judy saw that ominous dark clouds were beginning to blow in from the west. She nudged Alex and pointed.

'Look!' she said. 'Do you think we'll get rain?'

'Some time tonight, probably,' agreed Alex. 'But by then we'll be cosily tucked up in bed with other things on our minds.'

'Mmm,' said Judy, snuggling up against him. 'And what if it rains all day tomorrow?'

'Then we'll just have to stay indoors and play games,' replied Alex.

The rain held off for several hours. When they finally scrambled down from the waterfall track, footsore and dirty, they were able to drive to Hastings for a refreshing swim in the thermal pool. By the time she had washed her hair and changed, Judy was in the dreamy, relaxed state of exhaustion that came after a hard day in the open air.

'That was a perfect day!' she said with a sigh of pleasure, as Alex parked the car outside the lodge and held the door open for her.

'And it's not over yet,' he said in a voice full of meaning. 'I think we'll have a rest first, and then dinner.'

The next hour passed like a dream for both of them. When she finally lay back against the crisp broderie anglaise pillows and closed her eyes, Judy smiled a warm but wistful smile. In the bathroom, she could hear water running, and, if she forced her drowsy eyes open, she could just catch a glimpse of Alex's naked, tanned body as he soaped himself under the shower. She gave a little sigh. Their physical passion was overwhelming. Alex had just held her here in this very bed, bringing her to gasping point with pleasure, and his urgency had equalled her own. And yet emotionally they were still like strangers. She knew his body now as intimately as any woman could. But his feelings he kept a secret from her. And, if she tried to talk to him of love, it was as if a barrier came down between them, shutting her out. Her eyelids fluttered again. One day, she thought yearningly, one day . . .

'Sorry. Did I startle you?'

'You kissed me!' said Judy in astonishment. 'You stroked my hair.'

'You looked so nice lying there asleep that I couldn't resist it,' said Alex. 'Besides, you'll have to get up now if you want any dinner.'

'Mmm,' said Judy, yawning and stretching. 'Did you leave the shower on?'

'No, that's the rain,' said Alex. 'It started while you were asleep. Rather soothing really, isn't it?'

It poured all the way through dinner, and Judy decided Alex was right. The muted sound of the rain outside was soothing. It drummed on the tin roof and gurgled in the downpipes, and, since they were too tired to want to talk much, it gave them a comfortable excuse for silence. They ate grilled lobster with a French salad and once, when Alex was pouring the wine, their hands touched and they smiled at each other like conspirators. Judy was sorry to see the meal end, reluctant to lose the sense of closeness they felt.

'Shall we go out and sit on the veranda for a while?' she asked.

'Good idea,' agreed Alex

It was cool on the veranda, but not actually cold, and the west wing of the building sheltered them from the wind. Outside the landscape seemed to have changed dramatically since the morning. All the hills were swathed in scarves of mist, and the sky overhead was grey and leaden. Rain dripped from the boughs of the gum trees, and underneath a hedge a couple of currawongs huddled for shelter with their black feathers fluffed out.

'Aren't they sinister-looking birds?' said Judy. 'I had a book of *Grimm's Fairytales* when I was a kid, with a picture of ravens on the front. They looked just like those currawongs —huge and black and evil, just like an omen of disaster.'

Perhaps there was more truth in that than she realised, for ten minutes later, as they were about to go inside to the warmth of the fire, a car pulled up in the gravel car park outside. A tall figure dressed in a black japara and waterproof trousers scrambled out and came scurrying across to the building, head down against the rain.

'Poor chap! He'll be soaked,' said Judy, turning away to open the front door.

But something drew her gaze back. The newcomer was throwing off the wet hood of the japara, and Judy saw that it was not a man, as she had first supposed, but a girl. A girl, who was smiling a familiar, dazzling smile at Alex.

'Surprise!' said Stephanie.

Judy was so annoyed that for a moment she was tempted to step forward and tell Stephanie in no uncertain terms what she could do. But a new arrival restrained her. As she stood glaring at Stephanie, a short, wiry man bounded up the stairs between them and came to a halt, gazing in astonishment at Alex.

'Tom Cooper!' exclaimed Alex. 'What on earth are you doing here? I haven't seen you for years.'

'Alex! Good to see you, mate! I thought you'd gone to Canada.'

'I did but I'm back,' said Alex. 'Tom, I'd like you to meet my wife, Judy.'

'Hi, Judy.'

Judy felt her hand being shaken vigorously, and gazed into a pair of the warmest blue eyes she had ever seen. Her glance took in curly brown hair, a curly beard already slightly grizzled, and an engaging grin, and she knew at once that she liked Tom.

'Have you ever met Stephanie Hargreaves?' asked Tom. 'Oh, Alex. Sorry, mate, of course you have! You used to go out with her, didn't you? Well, that was years ago. Judy, do you know Stephanie?'

'Yes, we've met,' said Judy coolly.

'So, what are you doing down here?' continued Tom. 'It's the last place I'd expect to meet anyone I know.'

'Having a second honeymoon,' said Alex with a grin. 'Or, at least, we were, until you barged in.'

'You sly old dog!' said Tom. 'Well, don't worry, we won't keep you away from it for long. We've just come over for a few supplies, then we'll be getting back to the hut. They keep a little shop here at the lodge, you know. It's handy when you run out of things.'

'How about you?' asked Alex. 'What are you doing in this neck of the woods. Bushwalking?'

'No, mate. Caving. There's a whole new complex of caves that was discovered here only a couple of months ago, and, let me tell you, they are little beauties. They're mostly limestone, multi-chambered and really well decorated. Gours, straws, stalactites—you name it, they've got it. That's why I'm over here right now, actually. I took so many photos with my old Polaroid camera today that I've run out of film. And we're going into one of the best chambers tomorrow.'

'Sounds interesting,' said Alex. 'I'd like to hear more about it.'

'I'll tell you what,' said Tom, 'Just let me go inside and buy some more film before they close the shop, and then I'll come back out and tell you about it.'

'Perhaps Alex would like to come over to the hut and see your photos, Tom?' suggested Stephanie.

'Yeah. Great. Why don't you, mate? We're only a few hundred yards away, really. The only reason we drove over tonight was because old Steffie didn't want to ruin her hairdo.'

'Judy?' asked Alex deferentially. But he could hardly keep the enthusiasm out of his voice.

'Sure,' said Judy with a bright smile. 'Why not?'

Half an hour later Judy found herself perched on a wooden table with a steaming mug of coffee in her hands, watching while Alex and Tom sat talking animatedly amid a litter of maps and photographs. She glanced around her at the other cavers. Some were occupied reading books or checking their gear, their shadows huge and flickering on the firelit walls. Others were washing out socks and underwear, or drinking coffee by the fire while they discussed the day's caving. In different circumstances Judy would have loved it, for it reminded her strongly of bushwalking trips she had taken before Robin's birth. But now it was all spoilt by the presence of the tall, blonde girl who hovered beside Alex, waiting her chance to point out details in the photos or draw him into talk about the caves.

'Well, you're right, Tom,' said Alex at last, setting down his empty mug. 'They really seem to be something special. It's a shame we haven't got a few more days to spend here, or I'd be tempted to go down with you.'

'Why don't you?' said Tom eagerly. 'Look, mate, if you were thinking of going bushwalking tomorrow, you can forget it. I know these parts like the back of my hand, and I'm telling you now that cold front won't move off until Tuesday at the earliest. But once you're underground, what does it matter how much it pours?'

'Well——' began Alex. Then he caught sight of Judy's face,

which looked like a frozen mask. 'No, I couldn't, Tom. I don't have any gear.'

'Easiest thing in the world,' said Tom. 'We've got plenty of spare equipment. In fact, there's all Richard Pryor's kit—harness, overalls, helmet, the lot. He had to pull out at the last minute because he was called in to the hospital to anaesthetise an accident victim.'

'But what about Judy?' objected Alex.

Tom shrugged. 'Bring her along too, of course,' he said. He looked thoughtfully at Judy. 'She's a shrimp like me, so that's no problem. I'll tell you what, Judy, I'll go one better than Sir Walter Raleigh. I won't just lay down my cloak to save you from the mud, I'll lend you my trousers as well.'

Judy couldn't help laughing as Tom rummaged in a backpack, drew out a trim set of green overalls and laid them with a flourish at her feet, but in a moment she was serious again.

'I don't know, Alex,' she said. 'I've never been in a cave before. I might slow you down. And the whole idea makes me a bit nervous, to tell you the truth.'

A bit nervous, thought Judy to herself. That's the understatement of the year. It's all I can do not to scream with panic at the thought of going down underground, having all that weight of earth pressing over my head, feeling trapped and shut in. A bit nervous, indeed!

'Why don't you just stay on the surface, then, Judy?' asked Stephanie in a rather too eager voice. 'You could have a nice quiet day reading or something, while Alex looks at the caves.'

'Then again,' said Judy, her eyes flashing, 'it would be tremendously interesting, and it does seem a pity to waste the opportunity. Thank you, Tom. I'd love to come.'

'Attagirl!' said Tom. 'You'll love it. And, you know, there's really no need to feel nervous. Accidents are pretty

rare in caving. It's just that when they do happen, they tend
to be spectacular. Rockfalls, fractures, that sort of thing.'

'Rockfalls?' asked Judy faintly.

'That's right. Rockfalls are probably the biggest danger in
caving, because rocks can sit around underground in a highly
unstable state for a long time, until some poor unsuspecting
caver touches them and sets them off. And, of course, when
anyone does get injured, hypothermia is a real problem,
because the temperatures underground are so low. Lots of
times, it's not the injury that kills people, but the loss of body
heat. And then again, it's pretty difficult to get someone back
to the surface if they do get hurt. Probably the kindest thing
to do to someone seriously injured in a cave would just be to
shoot them right where they are.'

'Tom,' said Alex, rolling his eyes and making signs behind
Judy's back.

'Oh, sorry, Judy,' said Tom apologetically. 'I wasn't
upsetting you, was I?'

'No,' said Judy, swallowing. 'N-no. Of course not.'

'Good. Well, let's get you kitted out for tomorrow, then,'

Judy watched in alarm as Tom added thermal underwear,
a yellow miner's helmet with a light, a large torch and a
complicated pink harness to the overalls he had given her.

'What's the harness for?' she asked in a sinking voice.

'Oh, you'll need that if we go down any shafts.'

'Sh-shafts?' she faltered.

'That's right. Don't worry, you'll be quite safe. There's
been a tremendous improvement in caving gear since about
1970. These days, instead of ladders we use single-rope
techniques. To go down, you use a variable friction device so
that you can control the speed of your descent. Climbing up,
you'll use a type of cam, which can only slide up the rope
and not down. That's what the loops on your harness are for.
You move up one leg and slide up one of these cams, then

you move up the other leg and slide up the other cam. So you're actually walking up the rope like this and you can't possibly fall off, because the weight of your body locks the cam. It's dead simple.'

'Oh,' said Judy. 'Good.'

Yet, in spite of Tom's reassurance, she lay awake half the night, hoping desperately that it would be fine and sunny in the morning so that they could bow out of the caving excursion. But in vain. The first light that crept into their room at six o'clock was dim and grey, and throughout breakfast the rain dripped dismally off the shrubs outside the dining-room. When Tom's four-wheel-drive vehicle nosed into the car park, Judy had almost made up her mind to tell Alex how scared she was and back out of the trip, but the sight of Stephanie smiling mockingly brought back her resolve. Head held high, she stowed her pack and climbed in beside Alex.

There was a ten-kilometre drive along a gravel road, followed by another kilometre on foot before they came to the cave's entrance. The fissure in the rock was so well screened by trees and shrubs that Judy did not even see it, until Tom plunged into the undergrowth and disappeared.

'Come on, honey,' said Alex, his face alight with enthusiasm. 'You're going to enjoy every minute of this.'

Much to Judy's surprise, she found that, when her initial fear had worn off a bit, she was enjoying herself. At first there was little to see. A stream came bubbling out of the cave mouth, but the path which wound along next to it into the cave's interior was muddy and uninteresting. And, when she shone her torch on the cave walls, she saw only dark outcrops of rock. No glow-worms, no stalactites. Not even bats. But after five minutes' walking, Tom took a turn which led them away from the stream and into a downward passage, where the side walls moulded themselves into astonishing shapes, like the flying buttresses of a cathedral. To Judy's relief and pleasure, Alex was taking very good care of her. He had resisted Stephanie's attempts to claim him as an escort, and instead was shining his torch for Judy and stretching out his hand to help her over the rough spots. And, when they reached the end of the descent and came out into an open space, he put his arm around Judy and gave her a brief squeeze.

'This is where the good bit starts. Right, Tom?' he said.

'That's right,' agreed Tom. 'But let me just give you all a warning. You see that passage we've just come down? Well, there's another one just like it over here to the left. See where my torch is shining? That one leads into what we've called the Magic Lantern Cave, and I don't want any of you going in there. It's highly unstable, and there was a serious rockfall there only last week. Jerry nearly got his brains bashed in, didn't you, mate?'

'Yep,' agreed Jerry.

'Anyway,' continued Tom, 'most of you are experienced enough to know that things can be very confusing underground. It's easy to lose your sense of direction, and if an accident happens you may put other people's lives at risk as well as your own. So all I'm going to say is this. Stick together and take a damned good look at that entrance to the Magic Lantern Cave, so you won't wander into it by mistake when we're coming back. OK, end of sermon. Now we're going down into King Neptune's Cavern, and you'll really see something spectacular.'

Tom was right. Judy gazed around her in amazement at the strange and beautiful rock formations. The cave was aptly named, for there was a strong illusion of being underwater. She saw crystalline structures that looked like pale sea urchins, and odd formations for all the world like coral reefs, jutting out from the walls. Around each new bend there was some fresh wonder. Strangely shaped brown and amber rocks, stalactites resembling bamboo curtains strung across an opening in the cave wall, a shiny porous substance that seemed to flow across the cave floor like molten bread dough, stalagmites as graceful as Balinese temples. She was amazed, when Tom finally called a halt for lunch, to look at her watch and find that it was past one o'clock.

'Well, what do you think of it all?' asked Alex, slinging his pack on a convenient rock and searching for his lunch box.

'It's amazing,' admitted Judy. 'Really extraordinary—like another world.'

'Are you glad you came, then?' he asked.

'Yes, I suppose I am,' she admitted.

He smiled at her then, his helmet light sweeping down into her eyes and making her blink, and she touched him fleetingly on the arm before she turned to get her own lunch.

'Do either of you have a can opener?' asked a familiar voice.

Judy looked up to find Stephanie, gazing sweetly and helplessly at Alex, with a can of pineapple juice dangling from her fingers. To Judy's surprise, Alex snubbed this approach quite ruthlessly.

'No, sorry,' he said curtly, turning his back on the other girl. 'You'll have to ask someone else.'

He certainly was trying hard to keep his promise, Judy thought, stifling a grin as she watched Stephanie walk huffily away. But a few minutes later, when Judy was looking in another direction, Alex's gaze strayed wistfully to Stephanie and dwelt for a moment on the long, slender lines of her body. Stephanie caught that gaze and redoubled her efforts to attract Alex's attention. When they were packing up to leave, and Alex hesitated over a tangle of harness, her graceful, golden fingers were instantly beside his, sorting out the lines. And somehow, when the party formed into single file for the return journey, Stephanie manoeuvred herself into the place immediately in front of Alex, giving him ample opportunity to observe her as she climbed and wriggled her way ahead of him.

But this ploy was largely a failure. Alex was well aware that Stephanie was flirting with him, and he resented it, for Judy's sake, if not his own. Poor old Judy wasn't used to caves like the rest of them, and she was obviously tiring now, although she struggled hard to keep up. Alex thought it was in poor taste for Stephanie to keep flaunting her figure at him whenever she climbed over a rock, and he spent more time looking backwards and shining his torch to help Judy than admiring the bounty displayed in front of him.

Stephanie was not used to having her charms ignored, and she resented this offhanded treatment. Time was slipping away, and she had not yet succeeded in exchanging more than a few words with Alex, but before long she saw her opportunity. At three o'clock Tom called a halt for afternoon tea in the broad open area in front of the twin passages leading to the Magic Lantern Cave and the surface. The moment everyone was settled with thermos flasks and cups, Stephanie came picking her way delicately across the rocks towards Alex, holding out a tin of fruit-cake and smiling enchantingly.

'Fruit-cake, Alex?' she asked gaily. 'I know you can never resist fruit-cake.'

'Thanks, Steph,' said Alex, taking a slice of cake and turning immediately back to Tom. 'Now, where exactly do you think the other cave runs off? Through that fissure diagonally across from here?'

'Come on, mate, and I'll show you. That's easier than trying to explain. You see where that ledge is over to the left? Well, look just above there. No, higher . . .'

They lounged away, still carrying their coffee and totally engrossed in their conversation. Judy had to smother a grin at the chagrin on Stephanie's face, but there was no doubt that the other girl was resourceful. A moment later, as she was climbing gingerly back across the rocks, she let out a little gasp and slipped sideways.

'Are you OK, Stephanie?' asked Jerry.

'It's my ankle,' said Stephanie, sitting on a rock and smiling bravely as she examined it. 'I seem to have twisted it. I don't like to be a nuisance, but could you ask Alex to come and take a look at it?'

'I'll have a look at it, if you like,' said Judy in an amused voice, 'I'm a doctor too, remember.'

Stephanie cast her a look of pure poison. 'Thank you, Judy,' she said. 'But I'd rather have someone a bit more experienced, if you don't mind.'

'That's OK with me,' said Judy, shrugging. 'Hey, Alex! Come back here, can you? Stephanie wants you.'

'What for?' asked Alex in exasperation.

'She's twisted her ankle and she wants you to take a look at it.'

'All right. In a minute,' agreed Alex ungraciously. 'I'm busy at the moment.'

Stephanie stared across at his uncaring back in disbelief, and tears of anger and self-pity flooded into her beautiful eyes. In the past Alex had always come running at her slightest word. Now he was just ignoring her, the selfish, hateful pig! Well, she'd soon show him!

'Hey, you lot! Come and take a look at this!' called Tom. 'Alex has found something really interesting over here.'

The other cavers scrambled to their feet and made their way across to the corner of the cave, where Alex's torch was lighting up a breathtaking formation of stalactites. Out of the corner of her eye, Judy saw Stephanie limping off in the opposite direction, towards the twin passages.

'I'm going back up to the car!' called Stephanie petulantly. 'I just can't bear the pain of this ankle any longer.'

Nobody was listening except Judy, and she simply shrugged. Let Stephanie go and stew in the car for a while. It wouldn't do her any harm.

'Look! Look!' cried Tom on a rising note of excitement. 'Hey! There is a passage up here. Alex, give me a hoist up and I'll take a look!'

Judy joined the crowd in the corner, gazing up curiously at the dark opening in the rock above, but then something made her look back. What she saw made her forget all about passages in the rock and twisted ankles.

'Tom! Tom!' she called urgently, tugging on the leg of his overalls as he disappeared up the wall. 'Stephanie's taken the wrong fork. She's gone into the Magic Lantern Cave!'

They all turned at once, but it was too late. From the black archway in the cave wall came the loud, grinding rumble of falling rock, followed by a scream of genuine pain or terror. And then silence.

CHAPTER EIGHT

A CLOUD of choking dust and tiny stones sent them all reeling instinctively back, covering their eyes and mouths for protection. But the moment the rockfall had stopped, there was an instant flurry of action with people crowding round the entrance to the Magic Lantern Cave, babbling excitedly and grabbing at flashlights and ropes. One of the girls burst into tears, and several other people began shouting Stephanie's name. Above the uproar, Tom's voice rose firm and clear.

'Shut up, everybody. Alison, take it slowly, there's no need to cry yet. Now, the first thing is to find out how bad this really is.'

The voices rose excitedly again.

'She must be dead!'

'She couldn't possibly have survived it!'

'Just look at all that rubble.'

Tom raised his hands again, appealing for quiet. Then he shone his torch into the passageway. Someone gasped and they all stood staring in fascinated horror at what had happened. It was as if some giant had decided to tear the cave walls apart. Huge chunks of stone were wedged in the narrow passageway and the crevices between them were filled with rocks as large as cannon-balls. As they watched, a small shower of stones fell from high up and came rattling down to the floor like a burst of hail. It was horrible. Nobody could possibly be alive under all that. Judy gave a little, gulping sob.

'I should have stopped her!' she wailed. 'I saw her leaving, but I thought she was just going back up to the Land Rover.'

'Judy, wait!' cried Tom eagerly. 'This could be important. Did anyone else see Stephanie leave?'

138

There was a chorus of denials, accompanied by shrugs and head shaking. Tom set his hands firmly on Judy's shoulders.

'Listen, Judy,' he said, 'I want you to think really hard. How much time would you say elapsed between the moment Stephanie entered the passage and the time when you heard her scream?'

'I don't know,' said Judy slowly. 'About fifteen seconds, I suppose. Why?'

'Just this!' answered Tom, a note of excitement creeping into his voice. 'That passage is quite short —no more than ten metres or so—and then it opens out into a large cave. It's quite possible that Stephanie was able to run for it when she heard the rocks falling. She could be still alive inside there.'

They all stared at the apparently impenetrable rubble in front of them, and Jerry said what they were all thinking.

'Well, if she is, how the hell do we get her out of there?'

Tom was pacing around, chewing on his knuckles. 'First things first,' he said. 'This is probably going to be a major rescue exercise, so we'd better get help. Jerry, here. Take my car keys and drive down to the lodge. Notify Search and Rescue and tell them what's happened. Stay by the phone and, as soon as we have any more news here, I'll send somebody down in the other vehicle to update you. Got it? Right, the next thing to do is for us to try and find out what's going on here.'

'Do you think it's safe in this cavern?' asked Alex. 'Or should we send the girls back to the surface?'

Tom looked around thoughtfully.

'I think we're pretty right here, mate,' he said. 'What's worrying me is that little pile of goodies in the passageway. It's just possible that she's wedged somewhere underneath them, still alive. But they don't look too stable to me, and the slightest movement could bring them down on her completely. The other problem is that we don't have much time. It's three twenty-eight now. If she's injured, she won't last long without help. You know as well as I do, an ambulance will take two hours to get here from Hobart. We've got to try and find her ourselves.'

'How about that passageway you were exploring over in the corner?' asked Alison. 'Is there any chance that might lead through to the cave?'

'Good thinking,' said Tom. 'We'll go and have a look.'

While Tom and a couple of others were busy in the passage, Alex came over to Judy. Now that she was no longer moving about, she realised how cold and clammy the air was, and she began to shiver uncontrollably.

'Come on,' said Alex. 'What you want is something to occupy you. Help me check through this first-aid kit in case we need it soon.'

With cold fingers Judy began to go through the contents of the kit, checking off anything that seemed likely to be useful.

'One roll of adhesive plaster, two rolls of crêpe bandages, two No. 13 BPC standard dressings, two No. 14 BPC standard dressings, two compressed packs of St John triangular bandages, antiseptic solution, forceps, scissors, safety-pins, swab bowl, thermometer, space blanket, hypodermic syringe, morphine. There aren't any splints, Alex.'

'We can pull the frame of a backpack apart, if necessary,' said Alex.

Judy nodded, replacing everything carefully in the first-aid kit. She shook a can of insect repellant and found it was almost empty.

'Oh, well,' she said with a sigh. 'I don't suppose she'll be needing insect repellant anyway.'

She did not voice the thought which was growing steadily in her mind that Stephanie would not be needing anything they could offer her. There had been no sound from the Magic Lantern Cave after that first terrifying scream, and Tom had not come back with any news about another entrance to it. Would they all have to just stay down here in the cold and dark until it was too late even to hope? Judy shivered at the thought and Alex reached into the first-aid box, unwrapped the space blanket and draped it round her shoulders.

'Not much point in having you freeze to death,' he said. 'I might need your help before long.'

Judy looked up at him. The only light was the harsh beam of a torch set on a rock beside them, and it made Alex's face seem like a grim mask of hollows and lines. Hope and despair were obviously fighting within him, and Judy longed to reach out and touch him, but she did not dare. He loves her, she thought miserably. And she's probably going to die, is probably already dead. If only I'd stopped her, when she left. If only she hadn't taken the wrong turn by mistake. Or did she do it on purpose to get Alex's attention? Poor, stupid Stephanie!

Her thoughts were interrupted by an exclamation from Alex. As he leapt swiftly to his feet, she followed his gaze and saw Tom coming back from the far corner of the cavern. But hope died as fast as it rose, for Tom was shaking his head disgustedly.

'It was a dud, mate,' he said wearily. 'Didn't lead anywhere but into a dead end. Well, there's only one thing left to do.'

'What's that?' asked Alex.

Tom was drinking from a water bottle, and he swilled the liquid round and round in his throat and spat before he answered.

'Sorry, Judy,' he said. 'It's the dust. I'll have to go in, of course. See if I can find a way through the rubble.'

'That's crazy!' exclaimed Alex. 'That stuff could shift at any moment and come roaring down on top of you.'

Tom shrugged. 'It's her only chance,' he said.

'Then let me go!' exclaimed Alex.

'No, mate,' said Tom, taking another swig of water and grinning through the dust that caked his face. 'You've got a wife and kid. But don't worry—I'll be careful.'

Careful? How much use was it to be careful with tons of rubble poised like that above his head? Judy wondered, as she watched him flat on his face, wriggling into a cavity at the base of the rocks . It was dreadful watching him go into that tiny hole, like watching all her worst fears about caves come true.

'Wish me luck,' said Tom, his voice faint and muffled from inside the tunnel.

'Good luck,' they all whispered.

His body stayed there for a moment, dark and dense against the light that filtered back from his helmet, then he crawled into the blackness and disappeared. Hours seemed to pass before they heard him scuffling and swearing as he worked his way back along the tunnel, but Judy's watch showed that it was only eighteen minutes. Eager hands reached out to help him as he came squirming through the entrance.

'Whoo!' he exclaimed as they dragged him clear. 'That's a pretty tight fit!'

'But did you find her?' demanded Alex, grabbing the front of Tom's overalls.

'Yes, mate!' cried Tom, throwing his helmet exuberantly into the air and catching it again. 'And she's alive. What do you think of that?'

Alex let out a subdued whoop of delight and clapped Tom on the shoulder. Then he sobered up again. 'What sort of shape is she in?' he demanded. 'There's blood on your shirt. Is Stephanie——'

'Steady on,' begged Tom. 'Just give me a minute. Has anyone got a drink bottle handy? I swear I've been eating dirt all the way along that tunnel.'

Someone handed him a water canteen and he took a hasty swig on it.

'Right,' he continued. 'First of all, the blood's mine and it's nothing serious. Just a scraped knuckle. But Stephanie is hurt, although I'm not sure how badly. I found her backpack crushed under boulders at the other end of the tunnel, and for a minute I thought she was a goner. Then I heard someone moaning inside the main cave. She must have dropped the pack and run for it when the rockfall started, but she went clean over a steep drop and landed on a ledge about fifteen feet below. I shone my torch down on her and she babbled a bit, but I couldn't get much sense out of her. Still, I reckon I could get down to her if someone else can come in and belay me on a rope.'

'I'll come,' offered Alex instantly. 'If you could manage to let me down, I can treat her before you bring her up. What's the matter?'

Tom was shaking his head hopelessly. 'You'll never make it in, mate,' he said. 'That tunnel's a bloody tight fit, even for me. What I need is another one of the Seven Dwarves. Someone about my size.'

'How about me?' asked one of the cavers, a slight, red-haired man with a beard.

'Good on you, Dan,' said Tom approvingly. 'I reckon we're in business.'

'But she needs a doctor,' said Alex desperately. 'What if she's got spinal injuries or something like that? Moving her the wrong way could lead to paralysis.'

'I know that, Alex,' said Tom with a worried frown. 'But what choice do we have? She's been in there over an hour now, it's freezing cold and she's probably lost a fair bit of blood. Even if we wait for the emergency services people, they won't be able to get down that tunnel much better than we can. I'd say our best chance is for Dan and me to bring her out if we can. Then you can treat her here, and we'll carry her back up to the surface, and with luck we'll have her ready and waiting when the ambulance arrives.'

'Couldn't we move the rocks?' asked Alex unhappily. 'Manhandle them out of the way or jack some of them up with a car jack? Clear a wider passage somehow?'

'Look, mate, you'd need a front-end loader to shift some of those babies. And, if you try, you risk bringing the whole lot down, which isn't going to do us or Stephanie a whole lot of good. Now, come on, get a first-aid kit ready for us and Dan and I will take it through. Maybe you can sit by the tunnel mouth and shout directions to us or something. But let's get going.'

'Well, at least let me try and crawl through,' pleaded Alex. 'I might be able to make it.'

Tom shrugged. 'Please yourself,' he said heavily. 'Dan and I will get back in first. You try and follow.'

But it was useless. Judy waited in anxious silence as Alex disappeared into that horrible little cavity under the rocks. Minute after minute ticked by as she lay on her stomach, shining her torch into the tunnel and listening to the scraping of their boots on the rockfloor. A few feet in front of her the tunnel curved away out of sight, and she kept her eyes fixed desperately on the boulder that blocked her view. What if there was another rockfall while Alex was in the tunnel? Panic surged through her at the thought, then she heard a muffled exclamation followed by the welcome sight of Alex's walking boots coming backwards round the bend.

'Tom was right!' he said, as he backed out of the tunnel. 'It was just too narrow for me.'

Defeat and exhaustion showed in every line of his body as he straightened up.

'You did what you could,' said Judy timidly, laying one

hand on his sleeve to comfort him.

He punched one hand into the other in frustration.

'Not enough!' he said 'She needs a doctor, Judy. And I can't get in to her.'

It was then that the idea which had been forming slowly at the back of Judy's mind came to the surface. 'You can't,' she said slowly, almost unwillingly. 'But I could.'

'What do you mean?' demanded Alex.

'I'm a doctor too,' said Judy resolutely. 'And I'm a lot smaller than you. If Tom can get through that tunnel, I can too.'

As she spoke, she was putting on her miner's helmet, checking her harness, fighting down the panic that threatened to overwhelm her.

'Are you crazy, Judy?' demanded Alex, grabbing at her arm. 'You can't go in there. Think about Robin.'

'I am thinking about Robin,' wailed Judy. 'But I have to do it, Alex. I'm a doctor. Please don't stop me, I have to go before I get too frightened.'

Before he could collect his thoughts, she had flung herself into his arms in a swift hug, then dropped to the ground and squirmed away out of sight.

'Judy!' he called desperately. 'Judy, come back!'

Crawling through that tunnel in the rock was like a nightmare come true for Judy. Head down and teeth clenched, she dragged herself doggedly along, trying not to think of the huge weight of rock that hung poised above her head. Tom was right about the dirt. In places the tunnel was so low that she had to flatten her face right into the ground in order to move at all. Yellowish brown mud smeared her chin, and once a shower of pebbles rattled ominously on her helmet, making her whimper with fear. Memories of Alex and Robin swam unbidden into her mind. She saw Robin running down the hill at Princes Park, his hair ruffled by the wind and his face alight with laughter. And then there was

Alex kissing her passionately beside his parents' pool, with the sunlight darting up in ripples from the water. Sunlight. Judy held on to the thought of it as she made her way slowly and painfully down the dank, cold passage beneath the rocks. Her helmet sent a yellow beam ahead of her, but on either side of that glow the darkness lay deep and threatening.

Then something caught her eye, something so horrifying that she let out a gasp of dismay before she remembered what Tom had said. A backpack lay crushed under a boulder, with only a shred of bright orange nylon and a couple of inches of twisted metal framework still visible. What had Tom said? Something about finding the pack at the other end of the tunnel. Then she must be almost through. Grimly she put her head down and crawled on, only to run up against a dead end. Lifting her chin, she turned slowly from side to side and felt rock jar against her helmet. The beam of her light steadied dead ahead on a hole that looked no larger than a dinner plate.

'I don't believe it!' cried Judy aloud. 'It's impossible! Why didn't they tell me?'

Panic set in. Suddenly she felt like a rat in a trap and she began to babble with fear.

'Let me out! Let me out! Somebody let me out! I can't stand it!'

She was not aware of footsteps scrabbling over rock, of Tom's surprised exclamation, or indeed of anything at all until a hand came through that tiny hole and clasped her fingers. Then she gave a convulsive shudder and began to sob.

'Shh. It's OK, Judy. You'll be fine.'

'Oh, Tom. I'm trapped in here. I can't get out. I'll have to crawl backwards all the way down that rotten tunnel like Alex did.'

'No, you won't,' said Tom reassuringly. 'Now, come on, settle down. I told you it was a tight fit, but a little, teeny thing like you will have no trouble at all. Now, just do as Uncle Tom tells you and you'll be fine.'

'O-OK,' agreed Judy uncertainly.

'Right. Now head through first, then one arm. Wriggle a bit. Push, come on push. You can do better than that. That's the way. Now the other arm. Brace your legs against the wall. That's it! Terrific!'

With a sudden twist, Judy fought her way free and tumbled head first on to the cave floor at Tom's feet.

'What the hell are you doing here?' he asked disapprovingly as he helped her up. 'Alex must have been out of his mind to let you come through.'

'It's nothing to do with Alex,' she said hotly. 'It was my idea. And I've come to treat Stephanie, so you can just show me where she is, thank you very much.'

'All right, all right, keep your wool on,' said Tom in amusement. 'Come on and I'll show you. It's an amazing place, isn't it?'

As he spoke, he flashed his torch around the cave. It was a large, spacious cavern with beautiful formations on its ceiling and floor. Above them hung hundreds of pale stalactites like chandeliers, and immediately in front of them rose the huge stalagmite shaped like a lantern that gave the place its name. Judy was relieved to be out of the narrow stuffiness of the tunnel, but she was far too preoccupied to care about sightseeing. Already her mind was racing ahead to dressings and splints and, worst of all, a stretcher to get Stephanie out.

'How badly hurt is she?' she asked.

'I'm not sure,' said Tom. 'We think she's probably broken her arm. Dan's down with her. Hoy, Dan! Judy's here.'

The torch light travelled across the uneven surface of the cave floor, and suddenly plummeted over a steep drop. Involuntarily Judy stepped back a pace. Then she craned forward and peered at the two figures down below. Dan was crouching on the outer lip of a ledge, about fifteen feet down and no more than four feet wide. He was bending over Stephanie, who lay very still with her right arm splayed out at an unnatural angle from her body. Below them was a sheer drop of perhaps a further thirty feet to an underground river, which flowed away into the darkness beneath.

'Can you let me down to her?' asked Judy, a trifle breathlessly.

'Are you sure you want to go down there?' demanded Tom. 'If you make a false step, it's a long way to the bottom.'

'I didn't come all that way along your horrible tunnel to give up now,' retorted Judy tartly. 'Just let me down, will you? I'll be careful.'

'All right,' agreed Tom. 'I'll get the first-aid kit.'

Dangling from a rope thirty or forty feet above a sheer drop would normally have made Judy weak at the knees with terror, but, after the claustrophobia of the tunnel, it seemed almost like a game. She landed without mishap, and made her way cautiously along to where Dan sat with Stephanie. He had taken off his parka and wrapped it around her for warmth, but she kept throwing it off with a fretful movement of her left hand and moaning with pain. Judy opened the first-aid kit and, keeping well away from the edge, began a careful examination while Dan held the torch and watched her anxiously.

'Can you hear me, Stephanie?' asked Judy.

'Mmm,' murmured the injured girl.

'I'm just going to do some quick first-aid, and then we'll get you out of here. OK?'

Judy was astonished to hear how bright and cheerful her voice sounded. Just as if she were back in Casualty at St Thomas's with a stretcher and orderly on hand to whisk Stephanie away the moment she gave the word.

'OK,' replied Stephanie in a slurred voice.

Encouraged, Judy leant forward. 'Can you tell me where

you're hurt?' she asked.

'My arm. My—right—arm. Broken. Uh! Uh! Uh! Don't touch it.' Stephanie lay back against the parka which Dan had pillowed under her head and began to groan and whimper.

'It's all right, it's all right,' said Judy soothingly. 'You're going to be just fine. Hold the torch up a bit, please, Dan.'

'How bad is she?' asked Dan anxiously, when Judy had completed her initial examination.

'She's been lucky,' said Judy. 'It's really only a few cuts and bruises, and her arm, of course. I'm going to cut away her sleeve now, so I can take a proper look at it.'

While Dan held the torch, Judy cut gingerly at the fabric of Stephanie's shirt. A close look confirmed her suspicions. Stephanie's forearm was swollen and bent at an unusual angle, and there was extensive bruising in the centre of it. Gently Judy tried to straighten the limb, but as she did so she felt the bones grating. Stephanie let out a howl of pain.

'It's fractured,' said Judy, looking across at Dan. 'I'm going to have to splint it before we get her out of here, if I can. I've got morphine in the first-aid kit, and I can give her a shot of that to ease the pain, but I'll need something straight to use as a splint. Alex thought tubing from a backpack would do, but I'm not sure if he sent any through with Tom.'

'I'll find out,' said Dan.

'Hang on. Hold the torch and I'll give her the injection of morphine first. It'll take a while to go to work.'

Administering fifteen milligrams of morphine by intramuscular injection into the buttock was not a task that Judy would normally have thought very difficult. But with Stephanie squirming on a ledge above a thirty-foot drop, and the torchlight wavering wildly as she knocked Dan's arm, it proved to be quite a daunting task. When Judy was finally able to sit back on her heels with an empty syringe, she gave a sigh of relief.

'Right. A splint,' she said.

Luckily Alex had brought the dismantled frame of a backpack with him on his failed journey, and Tom was able to lower a bundle of tubing down to them. Once the anaesthetic had taken effect, Judy set to work to straighten the arm and bandage it in place with the splint. She then put it in a sling to elevate it, and tied the sling in place around Stephanie's neck.

'Well, I think that's it,' she said.

Dan lowered his torch with a sigh of relief. 'That was the hard bit,' he said. 'Now we get to the impossible bit—the journey back. Take a break for a minute, Judy, and I'll talk to Tom about how we're going to get her out.'

Judy stood up to ease her cramped limbs, and was surprised to find that she was trembling with exhaustion and reaction to all that had happened. The exertion of crawling through the tunnel had brought her out in a fiery lather of perspiration, but now her body was cooling. Her skin felt clammy and uncomfortable, and an anxious thought struck her. If she was cold, how must Stephanie be feeling after lying here immobile for so long? She crouched down again beside the semi-conscious girl and wrapped the space blanket more closely around her. A couple of feet away Dan was craning his neck as he held an earnest discussion with Tom up on the lip of the rock about rope techniques and the best way to raise an injured person. Judy's head swam, and to her surprise she found that she was shaking violently.

'Don't spend too long arguing about how you're going to get her up,' she warned. 'Just do it. She'll freeze if she stays here much longer.'

'All right,' agreed Tom. 'Come on. I'll hoist you up first and then Dan can help me with Stephanie.'

'No!' said Judy. 'Get her up first. She's freezing cold and I want her out of here as fast as possible.'

'But it'll take us ages to get her along the tunnel,' objected Tom. 'We'll have to drag her on a groundsheet or something.'

'It doesn't matter,' snapped Judy. 'I've got time to wait, but I'm not sure if she has. What's more, she's my patient and I'm not leaving till she's out. Now just move her, will you?'

Judy was almost relieved when they left. She heard Stephanie's agonised moans as they hoisted her up the cliff face, but she stopped her ears when they reached the tiny opening to the tunnel. It seemed impossible that they could ever squeeze an injured person through that minute space, and she didn't feel strong enough to listen as they tried. For a while there was no sound but the steady drumming of her own pulse beat, but when she finally unplugged her ears she could hear the distant scraping and cursing that showed they were inside the tunnel. With a sigh of relief she leant back against the cliff face. Dan had left his parka behind, and she put it on, revelling in its warmth, and tried to control the shaking of her limbs. What she had told Tom was not quite accurate. It was true enough that she was worried about Stephanie suffering from hypothermia, but there was another reason why Judy had not wanted to be brought out first. She simply couldn't face that awful tunnel. Even as a child she had always suffered from mild claustrophobia, had hated hide and seek in cupboards or under beds, had detested blind man's buff. But this wasn't mild claustrophobia. This was sheer, raging panic. She couldn't go back into that tunnel, not yet. And she didn't want Tom and Dan to see her cracking up and sobbing, not while they had a patient to attend to. Perhaps if she had a little rest, she would get control of herself. Judy put her head down on her knees and forced herself to take long, steady breaths, while she pushed back her fears of the dark. Instead she thought about sunlight. Sunlight and Alex.

Outside the entrance to the tunnel, Alex was pacing anxiously up and down. It was over an hour now since Judy had disappeared inside, and he had had plenty of time to think. The main thing he had been thinking about was what a fool he was. He should have stopped Judy, forbidden her to go. Anything might have happened to her in there. He knew from his own trip along the tunnel how desperately unstable it was, how likely to collapse without a moment's warning. At least that had not happened yet, but something else might have. He tried to force himself to stay calm and stop worrying, but it was impossible. Visions of Judy cold and lifeless or horribly mutilated kept flashing into his head. Of course, he was worried about Stephanie too. But somehow his chief feeling when he thought of Stephanie was annoyance. It was her stupid, childish behaviour that had caused this entire disaster. Judy's life was at risk, and all because of Stephanie. Try as he might, Alex could feel little sympathy for someone so foolhardy.

A scraping noise from the tunnel brought them all to the alert. There was some heavy breathing, followed by low, repetitive moans. Then slowly, inch by awkward inch, Tom's walking boots emerged backwards from the cavity in the rock. He knelt back on his heels and wiped the sweat off his forehead with the back of his hand before bending down again. As he tugged, the end of a groundsheet came into view and the other cavers sprang forward to help. Stephanie was dragged out, and someone pulled away the T-shirt which had been wrapped around her face to protect her from falling stones. She gave a strangled cough and stared around her, her eyes glazed with morphine. A moment later a weary, filthy Dan crawled out of the tunnel behind her, and staggered forward to lie gasping on the cave floor. There was nobody else.

'Judy?' demanded Alex, darting past him.

But, before he could fling himself down to look inside the cavity in the rock, there was a rattling sound and a shower of small stones rained down. A moment later came a muffled roar as the tunnel slowly collapsed.

CHAPTER NINE

ONCE the others had left her, Judy found that her main problem was keeping herself occupied while she waited. Her initial panic and claustrophobia had eased, but, when she hauled herself to her feet, her legs still felt weak and rubbery. She peered curiously over the side of the ledge at the river far below, but hastily decided that was a mistake. Instead she craned her neck and directed her helmet light up at the main part of the cave. That wasn't much better. Between the Magic Lantern stalagmite and the débris-filled tunnel was a pile of boulders she had scarcely noticed before. They were heaped up like rejects at a jumble sale, and looked ready to come hurtling down at any moment. On the whole, Judy thought, the wisest course was to sit down as close as possible to the cliff face, close her eyes and wait.

As she leant back, something hard and angular in the pocket of Dan's parka stuck into her. Exploring with her fingers, she found that it was a little container of peppermints. She shook a couple out into her palm and popped them into her mouth. Their hot, sweet taste was surprisingly refreshing, and she smiled reminiscently as her thoughts drifted back to the day she had first met Alex.

Officially she had been a second-year med student, but it was the very first time she had been let loose in a real hospital and she was already running late for a class. Bolting along an endless corridor, and cramming peppermints into her mouth, she had charged around a corner and run full pelt into him. Her peppermints had gone flying, along with Alex's clipboard and stethoscope. Even worse, a peppery charge sister with a trayful of drugs had only narrowly escaped being mown down as well. After his first startled exclamation, Alex had winked at her and taken on the role of peacemaker. It had taken all his charm to smooth the situation over, but in the end Sister Presgrave had accepted her apology and marched off, leaving Judy and Alex crawling around on the floor chasing peppermints like a couple of kids playing marbles.

Afterwards Judy had always smiled gratefully at him, and she had never been quite sure when the little surge of pleasure she had felt at meeting an ally had changed into something more. What she did know for certain was that she was hopelessly in love with him by the end of her second year. She knew perfectly well that he was unattainable, that he only smiled at her in the same way as he smiled at any other girl, and she did her best to put him out of her mind by going out with other men. But somehow no other man was quite like Alex Shaw. Nobody else had that teasing laugh, those dark, brooding good looks and powerful shoulders, that arrogant confidence. And certainly nobody else made her pulses race at the mere sight of him. When Alex announced his engagement to Stephanie Hargreaves, Judy was wounded to the core. Without that disastrous compound of jealousy and yearning, she would never have been swilling down rum and Coke so recklessly at that New Year's Eve party nearly five years ago, would never have found herself light-headed and reckless in Alex's arms after his row with Stephanie, would never have had Robin, would never have been married to Alex.

That thought made her pause. Well, I am married to him, she thought defiantly. I'm his wife, not Stephanie, and that's what really counts. No, it isn't, retorted a small voice inside her. Because it's Stephanie he loves, not you. Judy groaned, staring out into the darkness of the cave. She tried to hold on to the memories of the good times they had had together. The hours of hard work in the theatre and on ward rounds, the bushwalks, the games with Robin. But in the end it was useless, because the one image which remained uppermost in her mind was not of her and Alex at all. It was of a dark-haired man and a tall, blonde girl passionately kissing in the dim light of a cellar. Celeste might tell her to fight back, but the truth was that Stephanie had already won. Oh, Judy didn't doubt that Alex would keep his word and stay with her out of duty, but she wanted more than that. She wanted love. And Alex would never love her.

Making that admission was so painful that it caused her throat to ache and tears to fill her eyes. She huddled herself into a ball, burying her face in her knees and sniffing helplessly.

'It's over, Alex,' she whispered in a throbbing voice. 'It's all over now.'

As she spoke, a faint sound caught her attention, as if a floor board were creaking. Dully she glanced up, and felt her bones turn to water at what she saw. The huge mass of jumbled rocks that lay piled above her was slowly sliding down upon itself. For an instant, the rocks seemed to hang there frozen, then with a thunderous roar they plummeted towards her. Judy let out a single terrified scream and flung herself in against the cliff face. Stones showered over her, then something heavy struck her head and she knew no more.

When the tunnel leading to the outer cave collapsed, Alex went berserk. It took three men to restrain him from flinging himself inside as the rocks rained down, and, even when they had dragged him away to a safe distance, he continued to struggle and roar. Tom, clinging to his arm and yelling above the noise, had to shout his message several times before Alex would even begin to listen.

'What did you say?' demanded Alex at last.

'I've been trying to tell you, mate,' complained Tom. 'Judy wasn't in the tunnel. She was still inside the main cave on a ledge.'

'You mean she's not buried under all that?'

Alex's face went as white as paper as he gestured at the débris that filled the passage. This time there could be no question about it. Not even a mouse could be alive under that rubble.

'Look,' said Tom uneasily, 'I can't say how far the rockfall stretches, but there's a fair bet she's still sitting on the ledge in there, dusting herself off. She's probably not hurt at all.'

Relief rushed into Alex's face and was quickly replaced by fury. 'Thank goodness!' he exclaimed. 'But why the hell didn't you get her out before you brought Stephanie?'

Tom blew out his breath in a long sigh and spread his hands out. 'You're married to her!' he said 'You must know what she's like. It's worse than arguing with a bloody brick wall. "She's my patient and I'm not leaving till she's out. Now just move her, will you?"'

Alex's lips parted in a ghostly grin at this imitation of Judy in full cry.

'That sounds like her,' he admitted brokenly. 'But what on earth do we do now?'

Just as he spoke, there was an interruption as two men clad in blue and white uniforms came picking their way down the passage that led to the surface. They were carrying a stretcher and stumbling on the uneven floor of the cave.

'There's the ambulance blokes,' said Tom with undisguised relief. 'I'll just go and have a word with them. Maybe they'll know whether Search and Rescue are on the way. We're going to need digging equipment this time, for sure.'

As Tom made his way across the cave to the ambulance officers, Alex roused himself to examine Stephanie. Approvingly he noted Judy's treatment of the fractured forearm, but, the moment he was satisfied that no further medical treatment was necessary, he turned his back on her and walked away. Let the ambulance officers attend to her. Alex had more urgent matters to worry about. Tom came hurrying back across the cave, and Alex went anxiously forward to meet him.

'What did they say?' he demanded.

'The Search and Rescue team should be here within the next few minutes with proper digging equipment. The ambulance crew are going to take Stephanie back to Hobart, but they say they'll radio to have another ambulance diverted here in case Judy needs it. Oh, and the senior bloke wants to have a word with you about Stephanie's condition.'

Unwillingly Alex pulled himself away to talk to the ambulance officer. Any word or action which might help Judy commanded his immediate interest, but he did not want to waste any more time on Stephanie than he had to. His report to the ambulance officer was terse to the point of rudeness.

'There's nothing seriously wrong with her. A fractured forearm, a few superficial cuts and abrasions. No hypothermia to speak of. I'd say she'll be out of hospital by tomorrow morning.'

'Right,' said the ambulance officer, making a note on a pad. 'We'll get moving, then, and get out of your way. I'm sorry about your wife. I hope it all works out OK.'

Once the ambulance crew had departed, there was nothing left for Alex to do but wait for Search and Rescue. He longed for the relief of action, for a chance to lift boulders with his bare hands, to dig and burrow and labour in search of Judy. Anything at all to take his mind off the picture that kept haunting him, of his wife lying crushed and lifeless somewhere in the dark. The trouble was that, even when the Search and Rescue team arrived, there was little Alex could do to help them. Space was limited in the approach to the Magic Lantern Cave, and clearing away the débris required as much skill as strength. In the end he had to be content to sit fuming on an outcrop of rock, or pace restlessly round and round the cave, waiting for something to happen.

It was Tom who saw him through the endless, harrowing hours of that night. After a whispered consultation with the Search and Rescue team, the other cavers had decided they could do little to help by remaining. One by one, they had packed up and left, handing over packages of food and thermos flasks to Tom and Alex as a final offering of goodwill. When they had gone, there was nothing for Alex to do but wait and worry and think about Judy. And it was Tom who listened while Alex told him with pride about Judy's terrific cooking, and the herb garden she was planting in tubs on the back patio, and what a good doctor she was under pressure.

'Yeah, she's got guts, your missus,' agreed Tom. 'She's worth ten of that other stupid cow, if you ask me.'

'What do you mean?' asked Alex, startled.

'Stephanie!' said Tom scornfully. 'I suppose I shouldn't say it, seeing she's hurt and all that, but Stephanie's the one that got us into this mess. I know she's good-looking, but she's got no more brains than a Barbie doll.'

Alex reflected on that. He had a moment's mad impulse to leap to Stephanie's defence, but he thought of Judy and the impulse died.

'You're right, you know,' he agreed soberly.

'Oh, well,' said Tom philosophically, 'I suppose there always has to be one smart alec around who ruins things just when they're going well.'

'I suppose so,' said Alex uncomfortably. He was beginning to have the uneasy feeling that he might be just the same sort of smart alec himself. Things had been going so well for him and Judy. Yesterday on that walk, and later in bed . . . He shivered at the memory of her slender white body, the warmth of her kisses, the overwhelming desire they had shared. If only he had had the sense to run a mile when Stephanie had shown up.

'Well,' said Tom, smothering a yawn, 'I'm going to try and sleep for a few minutes if I can. You should get some rest too, you know. The blokes over there will call us as soon as anything happens.'

'All right,' agreed Alex unwillingly.

It seemed disloyal to sleep while Judy could be lying somewhere unconscious or freezing. But reason overcame his feelings and he crawled into a sleeping-bag and lay down. To his surprise, he found himself drifting into a doze that was half dream, half waking. He saw Judy holding out her arms to him, and smiling with that quirky little grin that sent dimples darting round her mouth and made her nose wrinkle so adorably.

'She's got a really cute nose, hasn't she?' he said.

'Who has?' demanded Tom drowsily.

'Judy, of course.'

'Oh, yeah. Too right.'

'I love her, you know, Tom. Isn't that terrible? I really love her, but I've never told her.'

'Then tell her, mate, tell her.'

It was after midnight when the shout came from the rescuers that brought them both stumbling out of their sleeping-bags and across the cave floor. One of the police workers held up a lantern and his grin flashed white in his dirty face.

'Well, we're through at the other end,' he said triumphantly. 'And we've cleared a fair-sized passage and braced the worst bits, so we should have her out pretty soon. You'd better get your gear and stand by, Doc.'

Afterwards Alex could never decide whether that was the best or worst moment of his life, when they dragged Judy clear on a stretcher. His heart almost stopped beating at the sight of her, for it was clear she was in a bad way. Her face was deathly white, her hair matted with blood, and there was a lump the size of an egg on her forehead. For a moment he stood frozen in anguish, realising with total clarity what it would mean to him if he lost her. The world seemed to stop dead as he bent forward and gazed longingly at her still features. Then, to his indescribable relief, he saw that she was still breathing. Suddenly everything began to move again as years of medical training took over.

'Hold the torch steady,' he ordered. 'I want to check these head injuries.'

His forehead creased into a worried frown as his fingers travelled over Judy's head. Luckily the scalp wound which had bled so freely was only superficial, and wouldn't need more than a few stitches, but he still couldn't rule out the possibility of brain damage from the blow on her head. Pulling open her eyelids, he shone a light into her pupils and let out a sigh of relief.

'What is it?' demanded Tom.

'I was afraid I'd find one dilated and the other normal, which would indicate internal haemorrhage and call for emergency surgery. But they're OK.'

'Then she'll be all right?' asked Tom eagerly.

'It's too soon to say for sure,' admitted Alex. 'I really need to see a CAT scan to find out what's going on. For the moment, the best we can do is patch her up and get her into hospital as fast as possible.' He turned to one of the ambulance officers. 'I'll give this head wound a quick dressing, then we'll put her neck in a soft collar and transport her in the coma position. And she'll need plenty of blankets to bring her temperature back up.'

The journey back to town was a nightmare for Alex. From the moment they stumbled out of the deep blackness of the caves into the moonlit clearing where the ambulance stood waiting, he was in a fever of impatience. The driver did his best and ignored all speed limits, roaring through tiny villages with his siren wailing and tearing along the country roads like a rally driver. But to Alex, fretting with impatience inside, it still seemed too slow. He felt he wanted to get out and push, or call for a helicopter. Judy lay peacefully throughout the journey, one leg drawn up and her head turned to the side, like a sleeping child. Too peacefully. Alex longed for her to wake, scream, moan. Anything to break that ominous silence. When the ambulance finally turned into Wellington Street and he saw the blurred outline of the 'Casualty' sign of St Thomas's hospital through the windows, he almost whooped with relief.

The casualty staff came rushing out to help the ambulance crew, and Alex saw the tall, blond figure of Richard Pryor striding towards him. Richard shook hands swiftly, clapped him on the shoulder and gazed anxiously down at Judy, who was being wheeled inside.

'Alison Farley rang and told me,' he said. 'Hell, Alex, I'm really sorry. How bad is she?'

'I don't know,' said Alex curtly. 'Let's get her admitted and find out.'

Within minutes Judy had been rushed through all the normal admission procedures and wheeled off to X-ray. The hospital grapevine seemed to be working at twice its usual power, and when Alex reached the CAT scanner he found one of the top neurosurgeons, Bob Price, already there, looking anxious and sympathetic.

'How long has she been unconscious?' he asked Alex.

'We don't know for sure,' said Alex. 'It's over two hours since they brought her out of the cave, so it's at least that long. But it's nearly eight hours since the actual rockfall, and she may have been knocked out when it first happened. Or she could have lost consciousness later. We just don't know.'

'Eight hours,' said Bob, wincing and shaking his head.

'What is it, Richard? What does it mean?' whispered a soft voice.

Alex turned his head vaguely and saw that Kate was standing clinging to Richard's arm. Her face looked pale and strained, and she was wearing an old tracksuit, obviously pulled on in haste. He wondered where she had sprung from, for he hadn't even noticed her before. Swallowing hard, he opened his mouth to try and explain, but found he just couldn't say the words.

'You tell her, Richard,' he said, turning back to the screen of the CAT scan.

'Any more than three hours or so of unconsciousness and you start to worry with a head injury,' said Richard gravely. 'If she doesn't come round soon, it could mean there's internal bleeding. Possibly brain damage.'

'Brain damage?' said Kate in horror. 'Oh, no. Not Judy.'

'Look at this!' exclaimed Bob jubilantly. 'I'll tell you what! This is better than I expected.'

The three doctors crowded round the screen, and Kate heard Alex give a distinct sigh of relief.

'Will somebody please tell me what's going on?' she begged.

'Come and see,' invited Richard. 'Look at this now. The scanner actually takes slices through the head, so it's rather like looking at a very detailed X-ray. What you can see here is a picture of the brain, and there's no sign of swelling or internal haemorrhage. And she doesn't have a fractured skull, which is really good.'

'She's not responding to stimuli, though,' said Alex in a worried voice.

'So what will you do now?' asked Kate fearfully.

'Put her in Intensive Care and observe her,' said Alex. 'And pray.'

'Alex,' said Kate. 'I know I'm not really hospital staff—well, not like a nurse, anyway—but could I come up and sit with her for a while? Judy's like a sister to me and, if anything happened to her . . . ' Her voice trailed away.

'I don't see why not,' he said hoarsely. 'I'll speak to the nurse on duty about it.'

Kate found the intensive-care unit overwhelming. Everything looked so strange and unfamiliar, more like a space station than a hospital ward. There were no windows, but bright lights blazed overhead, and a nurse sat at a desk containing so many monitors that it could have been the central computer control for a space-shuttle launch pad. Judy was transferred into one of the beds, and Kate watched unhappily as Alex repeated the now familiar battery of tests, shining lights into her eyes, pricking her with pins, trying to arouse some response. But there was nothing. He sighed and shook his head.

'I didn't really want to do this until I had something hopeful to say,' he admitted. 'But I can't put it off any longer. I'm just going to go and telephone her parents. Stay with her till I get back, will you, Kate? And, if there's any change——'

'Don't worry, Mr Shaw. We'll let you know immediately,' said the nurse on duty.

Left alone, Kate stared down at the tangle of electrodes and wires that covered Judy's body. It seemed as if everything imaginable was being monitored—heartbeat, temperature, venous pressure —- and yet none of the technology helped. Judy still lay there like a slumbering child, oblivious to everything around her.

What if she never wakes up? thought Kate, and a chill feeling settled in the pit of her stomach. Softly, barely aware of what she was doing, she began to talk.

'Jude,' she said softly, 'remember the day we started

school together? You were six years old and you had your hair tied in bunches, and the other kids teased you because your uniform was too big for you? And you punched Sean Reilly on the nose and got sent out of the classroom? And do you remember when we went to Devonport High School, and we got into trouble for wearing lipstick? And when we went to uni, and that old flat we had in Napoleon Street? Do you remember the day you met Alex?'

A faint sound caught Kate's attention. Suddenly she stopped talking, struck by an excitement so intense that she could hardly breathe.

'Nurse, come here!' she begged.

'What is it?' asked the nurse, coming down from her platform and bending over the bed.

'She sighed. I'm sure I heard her sigh. I was talking to her about Alex, her husband, and she gave a little sigh. Just like that! Ha!'

The nurse bent over Judy and examined her carefully, but there was no sound or flicker of movement.

'We'll try testing her responses to stimuli again,' she said briskly. 'Just a moment while I get my gear.'

They were both bending eagerly over Judy when Alex came back. He looked pale and haggard, and his gaze transfixed them almost accusingly.

'Any change?' he asked sharply.

The nurse looked up. 'Ms Wilson thought she heard her sigh, but she's still not responding to any stimuli,' she said doubtfully.

'What happened?' asked Alex, turning to Kate.

'Oh, Alex, I was talking to her. Just talking about things we'd done together, and then I mentioned your name and she sighed. I'm sure she did. Like somebody on the verge of waking up. Oh, Alex, talk to her, please. Maybe if she hears your voice it will do the trick!'

Alex knelt down beside the bed and took Judy's hand. He stared down at her blank face and tears sprang into his eyes. Hesitantly he glanced around the ward where four other patients lay sleeping, then he seemed to gather his resolve.

'Judy,' he whispered softly. 'Judy, please wake up and come back to me. I need you so badly. This is Alex, sweetheart. Don't leave me, please, please don't leave me. Judy, I love you!'

There was a faint sound, somewhere between a sigh and a groan. Judy's eyelids flickered and she swallowed. Alex, with tears running unashamedly down his cheeks, flung himself on to the bed and folded her into a crushing embrace, careless of the wires that coiled around her.

'Judy!'

She stirred and her lips moved soundlessly.

'What did you say, darling?' demanded Alex, leaning closer.

Then she spoke. And Alex thought he had never heard any sound more thrilling

'You're sitting on my leg,' she said.

CHAPTER TEN

THE distant sounds of early morning hospital routine filtered slowly into Judy's consciousness. The squeak of rubber-soled nurses' shoes on the floor, a far-off banging of a metal tray cover, the sound of a trolley drawing nearer. She sighed and stirred, then slipped back into sleep. Suddenly, quite close by, came the urgent sound of a beeper. In a flash Judy was up and groping for her clothes, wondering what emergency she was needed for. As she came fully awake, she became aware of two things. First that her head was aching ferociously, and second that a middle-aged nurse was holding back the curtain of the cubicle and staring at her reprovingly.

'And just where do you think you're going?' demanded the nurse.

'My beeper went. I'm on call. I have to . . .' Judy's voice trailed off as she looked around her. 'This isn't an intern's room,' she said in a puzzled voice.

'No. And you aren't on call either,' agreed the nurse. 'Now, just pop back into bed and let me tuck you up. Capering around out of bed with head injuries indeed! Mr Shaw will have a fit if he hears about this.'

'Mr Shaw?' said Judy. 'Has Alex been here?'

'He certainly has. He sat here for sixteen hours beside you after you were brought down from Intensive Care, and he'd still be here now, except that someone told him Nurse Hargreaves was looking for him and he shot off like a flash. Said he had something very important to tell her.'

'Oh,' said Judy in a small voice.

'Are you all right?' asked the nurse. 'You still look awfully pale. I believe you lost a lot of blood while you were down

166

in that cave.'

'Cave?' asked Judy.

'Yes. Don't you remember? Well, loss of memory is pretty common with head injuries. Perhaps it will come back to you later.'

'Did you say head injuries?' asked Judy.

'Yes. Here, take a look at yourself.'

Judy took the hand mirror that the nurse held out and stared at herself in astonishment. Her head was swathed in a huge white bandage, and there was a large, mottled bruise on her left cheek.

'Now, you just lie back and take things easy while I do your obs.,' said the nurse comfortingly. 'And then we'll get that husband of yours back to see you.'

Judy lay like a rag doll while the nurse checked her pupils, took her pulse and temperature and unwound the flex of a sphygmomanometer to test her blood-pressure. But she showed a flicker of interest as she heard the bleeps of the mercury running down.

'A hundred over seventy,' she said, 'My blood-pressure's never been that low before.'

'No, well, a few days' rest should soon set you right,' said the nurse cheerfully. 'Now, I've got orders to keep your lights down low and see that you get plenty of sleep. But it's nearly breakfast time, so would you like me to have something brought in for you?'

Judy made a face. 'I don't feel like food, thanks,' she said. 'And my head's spinning. I think I'd rather just go back to sleep.'

When the nurse had left, Judy huddled down under the covers and closed her eyes, but sleep escaped her. The talk about caves had jogged something in her memory, but, try as she might, she could only remember fragments of what had happened. She remembered Alex pacing around in agitation, shouting something about Stephanie needing a doctor, and she had a dreadfully vivid flash of herself crawling along some tunnel in the darkness. But why she was there or what had happened to her afterwards was a complete mystery. Her head whirled as if a cloud of butterflies were inside it. Then it settled on a single, devastating thought. Alex and Stephanie. What had the nurse said? 'Someone told him Nurse Hargreaves was looking for him and he shot off like a flash.' Judy bit her lip and turned her face into the pillow. What did it matter if she couldn't recall the details? The main facts were clear enough.

She was still lying motionless with her eyes closed a few minutes later when Alex's voice suddenly invaded the ward. Deep and vibrant, it overrode the clatter of breakfast trays and the soft gossiping of the other women.

'You said she'd woken, didn't you, Nurse Hughes?'

'Yes, Mr Shaw. And she spoke to me, although she seemed a bit confused at first. But when I left her, she was trying to get back to sleep.'

Judy heard the curtain being pulled aside, and part of her wanted to reach out for Alex and clutch him to her. But her head ached, and she felt she could not bear to hear him stammer out his explanations about Stephanie. So she lay very still and feigned sleep. She did not know that he was gazing down on her with an expression of profound tenderness an yearning, nor that he had just come away from telling Stephanie that he never wanted to see her again. She only knew that his hand rested lightly on hers for a moment, so lightly that she thought she had dreamt it, and then he moved away.

'I won't wake her,' he said in a voice that was rough with exhaustion. 'But tell her I'll be back later in the day to see her.'

The moment Alex had left, Judy regretted her cowardice in not speaking to him, but it was too late. All through the morning she drifted in and out of sleep, dimly aware of the chatter from other beds and the coming and going of nurses outside the curtains. But when she woke from a genuine sleep early in the afternoon, he was there beside her bed, sitting with his eyes closed and one hand up to his forehead. His face looked hollow and wretched, and there was a muscle twitching in his left cheek, which she recognised as a sign of tension.

'Alex?' she said cautiously.

His eyes flew open and a series of emotions seemed to flit across his face. Judy was not sure she could read them. Shock? Relief? Guilt? His hand came out and seized hers so powerfully that she cried out. 'Oh, Judy!' he exclaimed. 'Are you all right?'

'Mmm,' she agreed doubtfully. 'I feel a bit dizzy and strange, though.'

'That'll pass,' he assured her. He took a deep breath like someone preparing to dive off a ten metre tower, and then leant forward.

'Look, Judy,' he said urgently, 'this probably isn't the right time to broach the subject, but I have to talk to you about it. It's so desperately important, and I feel so guilty about it all. If I can't discuss it with you, I'll go crazy.'

'What is it?' asked Judy uneasily.

His eyes were unnaturally bright, as if he had fever, and, in his haste to speak, his words came tumbling out. 'I don't know how to say this the right way. I've hardly slept for two days now, and my head is just reeling with all that's happened, but I've got to explain it to you, make you understand.'

'Understand what?' asked Judy.

'About us. About Stephanie. You see, sometimes you don't realise until you nearly lose someone just how much you love them, how you feel as if life wouldn't be worth living if you lost them. And you've always been so nice, Judy, so loyal and understanding and supportive. I can't begin to tell you how

ashamed I am of the way I've treated you. But what I'm trying
to say is——'

'It's all right, Alex,' said Judy swallowing a sob. 'You
don't have to spell it all out to me. I understand.'

'Do you?' asked Alex searchingly, leaning forward and
gazing into her eyes with a tormented expression.

There was a sudden clattering of a trolley, and a nurse put
her head around the curtain. Judy swallowed miserably, feeling
grateful for the interruption. If Alex went on talking much
longer, she simply wouldn't be able to bear it, she would just
break down and howl like a baby. Oh, she couldn't blame him.
Obviously seeing Stephanie in danger had made it clear to Alex
where his loyalties really lay. But Judy still couldn't bear to lie
here and listen to him tell her all about it in heartbreaking detail.
She lay back patiently while the nurse checked her list and
brought her a little yellow tablet.

'There we are. Five milligrams of diazepam. I hope you're
not upsetting her, sir? She's supposed to be kept very quiet.'

'I'm a doctor,' retorted Alex irritably. 'I know all that. Is
there any chance we might get a bit of privacy to have a quiet
talk around this place?'

The nurse shrugged. 'Well, possibly tomorrow or
Wednesday,' she said. 'Mrs Shaw is due to be moved into a
private room as soon as one is available, but we're full up at
present. I'm sure I don't need to explain to you about bed
shortages.'

With that parting shot, she drew her trolley out between
the curtains and moved away. Alex turned back to Judy, but
found her huddled under the covers.

'Judy, can't we discuss this?' he begged in a low voice.

'Oh, Alex, there's nothing to discuss!' she said desperately.
'Look, I understand everything that you're telling me, but I'm
sure you must know how I feel about Stephanie. And I can
see as well as you can that there's no future for our marriage.

None at all. It's just too late and everything's gone wrong. Now, will you please go away and leave me alone? My head's aching and I feel terrible.'

Alex made one last futile movement with his hand, as if he were about to protest, then he nodded slowly. His shoulders sagged as he moved away from the bed. Hesitating, he turned back and saw her curled up, her chestnut hair escaping from the bandage and her face turned resolutely away from him. She seemed unbearably fragile, unbearably dear.

'Goodbye, Judy,' he whispered.

Later in the morning, Kate Wilson was outside her house when Alex drove up. He caught sight of her and pulled up.

'Kate!' he hailed her. 'Have you got a minute?'

She came hastily across the road. 'How's Judy?' she asked, as Alex climbed out of his car.

'She's doing well,' he said dully. 'She should be out of hospital in a few days.'

'Then what's the matter? You look terrible.'

'I — oh, hell! It's a long story.'

'Well, come inside and tell me over a cup of coffee. Richard's in there.'

Alex pulled a face and ran his hand over his unshaven chin. 'I can't,' he said simply. 'I can't face people at the moment.'

'Then come down the street to the park and tell me about it there. Maybe I can help.'

Five minutes later they were sitting in the park overlooking the blue waters of the river. Children ran laughing over the green lawns, and a pair of young lovers strolled hand in hand under the oak trees. Alex glanced at them and sighed.

'Right,' said Kate ruthlessly, pulling him down on to a bench. 'Now, what's it all about?'

'It's Judy,' replied Alex. 'She just told me our marriage is over.'

'Judy told you that?' demanded Kate incredulously.

Alex nodded. 'I wanted to ask you to help me,' he said. 'You see, Kate, I've got to leave Tasmania. I just can't bear to stay here at St Thomas's any more, if Judy and I are apart. I really love her, you know, and it would be sheer torture running into her all the time at the hospital.'

'So what are you going to do?' demanded Kate.

'I'm going off to Melbourne tonight. I have some holiday leave I was going to take over Christmas anyway, but I won't be coming back. The only thing is that I can't bear to break the news to Robin. I wondered if you could tell him for me. Oh, and there's this little note for the psychologist at work about a family that needs counselling. Judy's been worrying about them. Can you pass it on for me?'

'Melbourne?' said Kate. 'What are you going to do in Melbourne?'

Alex drew a long, shuddering breath. 'Well, to tell you the truth,' he said, 'I think I'm going to just chuck in medicine entirely and go to work for my father. Being a doctor was what I always wanted, and sharing it all with Judy was tremendous. But somehow, without her, it just won't mean anything any more. Nothing will.'

'Now, wait a minute,' said Kate. 'I can't believe I'm hearing all this. Are you absolutely sure that Judy said your marriage was over?'

'Absolutely,' agreed Alex glumly. 'No question about it.'

'But it doesn't make sense!' Kate burst out. 'I happen to know that Judy has been in love with you for years.'

'She has?' asked Alex doubtfully.

'Yes! And, what's more, she went off on that weekend trip with you hoping that it would bring you closer together.'

'Did she really?'

'Of course she did!' said Kate impatiently. 'So what on earth have you said to her today to make her want to divorce you?'

'Nothing!' said Alex indignantly. 'I just went into the hospital to tell her how much I loved her, and how sorry I was about all that stuff with Stephanie, and she told me to get lost. Honestly!'

'Are you sure, Alex? You must have made an awful mess of telling her, then! What exactly did you say to her?'

A look of strain came over Alex's face as he tried to remember. 'Well, I don't know what my exact words were,' he said slowly. 'But I said I wanted to tell her how I felt about her. And about Stephanie. And then I said that sometimes you don't realise how much you care about someone until they're in danger. And then some stupid nurse came in with a trolley and, before I knew it, Judy was telling me our marriage was over.'

'I see,' said Kate slowly. 'Alex, has it occurred to you that maybe Judy misunderstood you?'

'What do you mean?' demanded Alex.

'Look,' said Kate, 'I'm not a betting person, but I'll bet you ten to one that Judy thought you were talking about Stephanie when you gave her all that rigmarole about not knowing how much you loved someone until they were in danger.'

Alex look dismayed, and then, like the sun struggling out from behind a cloud, a smile crept over his face.

'Do you really think so, Kate?' he asked.

'Well, I think you ought to find out, anyway,' said Kate, smiling back at him. 'Come with Richard and me back to the hospital, if you like. We've got something special in the boot of the car that we were planning to take in to Judy anyway. Something we thought might cheer her up.'

* * *

Half an hour later the occupants of Women's Surgical Ward 502 were startled by the entrance of a tall, handsome man who bore very little resemblance to the exhausted creature who had been there in the morning. Alex had showered and shaved, and was smartly dressed in a beige linen safari suit and Italian leather shoes. On one arm he carried a bunch of fragrant Cecil Brunner roses from Kate's garden, and his eyes were alight with confidence and determination. But as he stopped in the centre of the room and saw the empty bed where Judy had been, his face went suddenly ashen.

'Where's my wife?' he demanded in panic.

An old lady who was knitting a bed jacket glanced up shrewdly and took pity on him. 'Now don't you go upsetting yourself, lovey,' she advised. 'Nothing terrible's happened to your wife. She's just been took over to a private room, like you was asking for this morning.'

'Where?' demanded Alex.

The old lady furrowed her brow and her lips moved soundlessly as she counted stitches. 'Room 517, I think they said. Or was it 527? You'd better ask one of the nurses.'

But Alex was already off. He wove in and out of hospital orderlies and dawdling visitors like an impatient motorcyclist in heavy traffic, and, when he came to the last corridor and found it almost deserted, he broke into a run. Sister Presgrave came out of her office and pursed her lips disapprovingly, but she was too late to stop him as he sped by. The moment he came in sight of Room 517, he grabbed the arm of a young nurse who was passing by and pointed at the door.

'Is Judy Shaw in there?' he demanded.

'Y-yes!' stammered the nurse.

'Right!' said Alex. 'Well, this time she's had it!'

Judy was lying miserably against a pile of pillows and staring at the walls when the door was flung suddenly open and Alex burst in. She started up with a cry of surprise, but immediately found herself being pushed back and ruthlessly kissed. For a moment she struggled. Then she gave way to the joy that washed through her in waves as Alex's mouth explored hers with passionate sweetness. He was holding her with such crushing force that she could scarcely breathe, but she was not even sure that she wanted to. His powerful arms felt so strong and safe around her, and the wild beating of his heart against her told her all that she needed to know. When at last he released her, she smiled shakily and sat back amid a flurry of pink rose petals.

'I brought you some flowers,' said Alex.

'So I see!' agreed Judy.

'Well, never mind the flowers!' said Alex, cheerfully throwing the mangled bouquet across the room. 'What I really want to say is this. Darling Judy, I love you more than anyone in the whole world and I simply can't live without you. So will you please, please stay with me and never leave me?'

'Are you serious?' asked Judy with a catch in her voice.

'More serious than I've ever been in my life, my dearest love,' said Alex earnestly.

'But what about Stephanie?' demanded Judy.

'If I never see Stephanie again, it will still be too soon for me,' he assured her.

'That wasn't what you said this morning,' protested Judy.

'Yes, it was!' said Alex, giving her a little shake. 'We had our wires crossed, Judy. Very badly indeed. What I was really trying to tell you was that seeing *you* in danger made me realise how much I love *you*. Because I do, you know.'

'Truly?' asked Judy.

'Truly,' agreed Alex.

'I thought you were still in love with Stephanie,' she confessed. 'I still don't remember properly what happened, but I know you were frantic about her.'

'That's true,' admitted Alex. 'Although I think I would

have been frantic about anyone disappearing like that. It was all so horrible. But when I really went to pieces was when I found you were trapped. I began to think of all the things we'd done together and I remembered all sorts of silly things about you.'

'What sort of things?' asked Judy shyly.

'Oh, the cute way your nose wrinkles up when you smile. Yes, just like that! And the way you sit around watching those sloppy old movies and crying when you think I'm not looking. And the way your face lights up when Robin comes into our room in the morning. And the kind of person you are. You never back down from a challenge, do you? Battling through med school, standing up to my father, rescuing Stephanie. However tough it is, you always go in with your boots on. And I just couldn't bear to think that I might lose you, that it might already be too late. When they brought you out alive, I just felt—Oh Judy. How can I ever explain what I felt? I've never been good at making speeches. All I can say is that we belong together. And I do love you. More than I ever thought possible.'

She seemed to have developed a strange interest in the top button of his safari suit, so that he had to put his fingers under her chin and raise her face gently so that he could kiss her. And then kiss her again. With a little sigh, she nestled contentedly into the curve of his shoulder, so that he was able to gaze down affectionately on her curly chestnut hair and her slender, perfect body.

'Those hospital gowns are awfully ugly,' he said teasingly. 'I wish you'd let me take it off.'

'Alex!' she exclaimed in a scandalised voice, and he was delighted to see that he had made her blush.

'I was just joking,' he admitted. 'But when you're out of here, it'll be a different story. For the time being, I'll just have to remember that you're a hospital patient.'

Yet, in spite of this resolution, Judy found that his fingers were straying down over her shoulders and arms, doing the most delicious things to her skin and making her pulse-rate quite wild with excitement. She raised her mouth to his, and found that his kisses were long, lingering and tender.

'Is this a standard method of treatment, Mr Shaw?' she asked in her best young doctor tones.

'That's right,' agreed Alex crisply. 'Guaranteed to bring about a complete recovery in a very short time.'

'Then I'll have some more,' she ordered blissfully.

They were silent for quite a long time, and when they finally drew apart Alex pressed his hand lovingly to her cheek.

'You haven't answered my question yet,' he said.

'What question?' asked Judy vaguely.

'Will you stay with me?'

'Well, of course I will,' she said, her voice brimming with happiness. 'I love you, you know.'

'Say that again,' begged Alex.

'I love you,' said Judy shyly.

'Oh, Judy,' said Alex, crushing her to him again. 'I want to ask you something else. I know it sounds silly, but I'd still like to know. But first of all, you'll have to pretend something for me.'

'What?' asked Judy, puzzled.

'Pretend it's five years ago, and there's no Stephanie and no Robin. Just the two of us. And I'm asking you this question. Will you marry me, Judith Lacey?'

'Oh, Alex!' said Judy, melting into his arms. 'Yes.'

They were still holding hands and gazing at each other when they heard a smothered giggle outside the door, followed by a perfunctory knock.

'That's Kate's voice!' said Judy. 'Come in, Kate!'

There was a bump and a muffled exclamation, then the door swung halfway open, stuck for a moment and then opened fully to reveal an extraordinary sight. Kate and Richard were pushing a wheelchair containing an occupant who must surely have been one of the most unusual visitors ever admitted to the women's surgical wing. Mr Ossi the skeleton was sitting bolt upright in the chair, nattily rigged out in Alex's best Italian pyjamas and Pierre Cardin dressing-gown. His bony skull was wrapped in a bandage identical to Judy's, and on his lap he clutched a brightly coloured parcel bearing a placard that said 'Get Well, Judy'. It was fully half a minute before Alex and Judy stopped staring at this apparition and found their voices.

'Those are my best pyjamas!' said Alex wrathfully.

'How did you ever dare?' asked Judy in an awed voice. 'You must have had to bring him right past Sister Presgrave's office!'

'Yes, we did!' agreed Richard. 'And she saw us too, worse luck! But it's OK, Alex. We told her it was one of your patients and you'd asked to see him.'

'You pair of lunatics!' said Alex severely. 'It'll be a miracle if I don't get dismissed from this place.'

'Well, that shouldn't worry you!' retorted Kate pertly. 'Considering you were planning on leaving medicine forever only this morning!'

'Oh, Alex, you weren't!' exclaimed Judy. 'What on earth for?'

Alex looked embarrassed and then cleared his throat. 'I couldn't bear to stay at St Thomas's if I wasn't with you,' he said, his eyes kindling as they rested on Judy. 'And I thought leaving medicine was the best way of punishing myself for being stupid enough to lose you.'

'But you haven't lost her, have you?' demanded Kate, looking searchingly from one of them to the other. 'You are staying together, aren't you?'

Alex looked down at Judy with a hint of a question in his eyes, but what he saw in her face evidently reassured him, for he sat on the edge of the bed and took her hand firmly in his. Then, clasping it as reverently as if it belonged to a queen, he raised it to his lips and kissed her fingers.

'No, I haven't lost her, Kate!' he said, his voice husky with emotion. 'And all I can say is this. If I have anything to do with it, Judy and I will be staying together forever.'

CHAPTER ELEVEN

JUDY was still in hospital when Christmas Day arrived, but with a little ingenuity the day turned into one of the best celebrations she had ever had. Alex arrived early with Robin, who was clutching an armful of his favourite presents and bursting with excitement,

'Hello, Mummy! Daddy says I have to kiss you very carefully so I won't hurt your poor head. There! That didn't hurt, did it? Except where I put my elbow in your eye?'

'No, darling, it didn't hurt,' Judy reassured him.

'Good. Guess what? I saw Father Christmas last night!'

'Did you, Robin? How exciting! What did he look like?'

'Oh, you know! He had a red suit and a long white beard, and he was wearing slippers just like Daddy's. I stayed awake specially just so I could see him.'

'Till three o'clock in the morning!' confirmed Alex drily.

'My goodness!' said Judy. 'And did he bring you lots of presents?'

'Oh, yes!' agreed Robin cheerfully. 'But he was pretty cross with me.'

'Why?' demanded Judy, casting Alex a look of inquiry.

'Because when he came into my room and started putting the presents down, I suddenly sat up in bed and shouted 'Boo!' and then he tripped over one of my toys and hurt his wrist.'

'Did he?' asked Judy sympathetically.

'Yes, and he said a very naughty word. You know, that one you told me not to say that starts with——'

'Robin!' said Alex sharply. 'Why don't you get down and play with your presents now?'

Robin pouted. 'I haven't finished showing them to Mummy,' he complained.

'All right. But hurry up about it,' commanded Alex.

All the time that Robin was demonstrating how his toys walked, talked, shot laser beams, dropped gobs of slimy plastic on the sheets and came apart into tiny fragments, Judy and Alex were gazing longingly at each other above his head. It was a relief to both of them when their son disappeared into a corner next to the washbasin with a toy car, but, before they could really begin to talk, a maid came in with Judy's breakfast on a tray. And after that the telephone rang, with Judy's parents and brother wanting to wish her a merry Christmas.

The rest of the day flew by in the same frantic way, full of interruptions and noise. It was a happy time for both of them, and yet completely devoid of the thing which would have given them the greatest happiness of all: time alone together. First there were presents to be opened. Alex had bought Judy a beautiful emerald bracelet to match her engagement ring, and there was a large box from Celeste and a smaller one from Yuri. Celeste's gift turned out to be a staggeringly expensive French nightdress, consisting of a thin film of pure silk with a few strategically placed scraps of lace, while Yuri's was even more remarkable. On the outside was a card which said simply, 'To the only woman in Australia who is a bigger bossy boots than my wife. With love from Yuri. PS I've lost five kilos.' Inside the box was a set of car keys for a brand new luxury Saab. When Alex told her the car was waiting at home in the driveway for her, Judy almost had a relapse from shock.

And after the presents there were the visitors to contend with. Kate and Richard and Tamsin came in first, with Kate blushing and stammering so oddly that Judy's gaze flew instantly to her ring finger and she was able to cry triumphantly, 'I knew it! Oh, Kate, congratulations! It's wonderful.' Afterwards Tom Cooper and Dan Southerby called in to see how she was recovering from her ordeal in the cave, and then there was a visit from the Burrows family, who had heard about the accident on the news and just had to come and check that Judy was really all right. Michael was still pale, but grinned cheerfully and held up a football, exclaiming, 'Look what Dad gave me!' and as they left, Mrs Burrows gave Judy a triumphant thumbs up behind her husband's back. And, of course, when they had gone, there was Christmas dinner to eat and more friends to see.

It was seven o'clock in the evening before Alex and Judy had a moment's peace. When the last visitor had departed, Alex ruthlessly barricaded the door with a chair and sat down beside Judy's bed.

'I'm sick of this!' he said. 'This place is such a madhouse that I need an appointment just to speak to you.'

'Never mind,' said Judy comfortingly. 'I'll be coming out of hospital tomorrow, and you've got your holiday leave now, although I suppose I'll have to go back to work pretty soon.'

'Oh, no, you won't!' said Alex triumphantly. 'I've spoken to Prof Castle and told him you need at least another two weeks off to recover. And *Maman* is taking Robin back to Melbourne with her tomorrow to give you a break. So we're going to be alone together at last, even if I have to disconnect the phone and put barbed-wire barricades along the front fence to do it!'

'It sounds wonderful,' said Judy.

It was wonderful. At last everything had slipped into place and Judy had the marriage she had always dreamt about. In many ways, it was even better than their honeymoon. There were long, lazy mornings in bed with croissants and coffee, walks along the beach with their arms twined around each other, candle-lit dinners in expensive restaurants. But at night there was also the pleasure of coming home to their own cosy house, of talking or reading, or just sitting quietly together without anyone else to interrupt them. Best of all, there was time for her to enjoy being married to Alex. And, even if he wasn't sentimental as she was, and didn't cling to memories or talk much about his feelings, his arms were warm and powerful around her every night, and she now had the happy certainty that she was loved. All in all, thought Judy, her life was as close to perfect as it was ever likely to be.

Of course, it was too much to expect that the rest of the world would never intrude on them. At about ten o'clock on New Year's Eve, just as Judy was planning a quiet supper and perhaps a moonlight stroll down to the harbour, the phone rang for Alex. Judy heard the low murmur of voices, then he hurried back into the living-room, pulling on his sports jacket as he moved.

'Sorry, Judy!' he said. 'It's an emergency. There's a baby with a tracheo-oesophageal fistula. I've got to get down to the hospital as fast as possible.'

'Oh, no!' said Judy, thrusting his car keys into his hand. 'Poor little thing. I do hope you can save it!'

He was halfway out the back door before a thought struck him. 'Why don't you come along and observe the op?' he said. 'I'm sure you'd find it useful.'

Judy didn't waste any time. She had snatched her handbag and was already in the car before Alex had even finished opening the gates. When they reached the hospital, Alex parked the car in his reserved space and they both sprinted inside. Sister Watson was waiting for them as they arrived panting to scrub up.

'Dr Pryor's already anaesthetised the child, Mr Shaw,' she said. 'And we're ready as soon as you are.'

Judy's heart turned over with pity and tenderness at the sight of the tiny baby lying on its side on the operating table, but before long professional curiosity took over and she watched in total absorption as Alex and his assistant worked. He swabbed the child's chest, draped it with sterile drapes and made an incision with a scalpel. Once he had retracted the ribs apart and his assistant had retracted the lung out of the way, Alex used a pair of scissors and forceps to dissect down to the fistula and then divided it. Scarcely breathing, Judy peered forward as the scrub nurse gave Alex a needle mounted on a needle-holder and a pair of forceps, and he went to work repairing the defects in the oesophagus and trachea. After that, it was just a matter of inserting a chest drain, then closing the ribs with a nylon suture, the muscle with a catgut suture, and the skin with another lot of nylon. To her surprise, Judy found that she was just as tired from watching as if she had been operating herself.

It was nearly midnight when they all emerged into the car park again. In spite of her exhaustion, Judy felt as if she were walking on air.

'He's going to be all right, isn't he, Alex?' she demanded.

Alex smiled and ruffled her hair. 'Well, he doesn't have pneumonia and he's well nourished. I'd say he'll be fine,' he said. 'Wouldn't you Richard?'

'Yeah,' agreed Richard, stretching himself. 'Whoo! Why don't you two come over to my place for a quick drink to celebrate the New Year?'

'Sorry,' said Alex swiftly. 'Judy and I are already going to a special New Year's party.'

'Oh, that's too bad!' said Richard. 'Well, some other time, then. Goodnight.'

'Goodnight,' replied Alex

'Alex,' said Judy in a puzzled tone as Richard disappeared across the car park. 'What party?'

'Ah, you'll see,' said Alex mysteriously. 'Just something I organised.'

'But my feet are killing me and I'm tired, Alex. Do I have to come?'

'Yes,' said Alex simply. 'Now, shut up and hop in the car.'

But when Alex started the engine, it gave a dismal splutter and then died. He stared down at the dashboard in annoyance.

'What on earth can it be?' he said. 'Spark plugs, flat battery, carburettor?'

'It's so nice to have a Mercedes' said Judy sweetly. 'You always know you can rely on them.'

'Judy—' began Alex warningly.

'I'll bet I know what it is,' she said, stifling a giggle.

'What?'

'When did you last put petrol in this car, Alex?'

Alex groaned 'We'll have to get a lift with Richard,' he said.

Just as he spoke, Richard's car came slowly past them. Alex blew his horn urgently and gave a desperate wave. Richard blew a sharp toot back, waved his hand and drove off.

'That moron!' said Alex bitterly. 'Shall I call the RAC?'

'No,' said Judy. 'It's a fine evening. Let's walk. You can pick up the car tomorrow.'

Secretly she was rather pleased. She had hoped for a stroll around the docks, where a riotous crowd was welcoming the New Year, and now she would get it. And, with a bit of luck, by the time they reached home Alex would have forgotten all about that silly party.

Just as they reached the waterfront, the whole place seemed to go crazy. Car horns began blaring, fireworks shot into the air and exploded in red and green cascades, people in the streets started dancing in conga lines and floodlights spilt across the dark water. Judy looked at her watch.

'Twelve o'clock on the dot!' she confirmed.

'Then we'd better celebrate! Happy New Year, darling!' He flung his arms around her, kissed her warmly and then dragged her, giggling and protesting, into one of the conga lines that was snaking around the waterfront. Down below them the yachts from the Sydney to Hobart race bobbed on the surface of Constitution Dock, and once Judy stumbled so badly that she was afraid she would go hurtling down on to somebody's deck or, worse still, land with a splash in the dark water. A vivid flash came back to her of that evening five years before when she had walked along here with Alex's arm around her and her legs feeling rubbery and strangely faraway. That was the evening when Robin had been conceived and, although she had not known it at the time, her whole life had changed. For a moment she was tempted to share the memory with Alex, but only for a moment. Alex would only laugh at her about it, and she did not feel she could face that. Suddenly the conga line disintegrated and they found themselves in the comparative quiet and darkness of Dunn Street.

'Home?' asked Alex.

'Home,' she agreed contentedly.

It was lovely to walk down the little brick path, to smell the jasmine that hung over the porch, to turn the key in the front door and know she was alone with Alex. Judy stifled a yawn and switched on the bedroom light.

'What should I wear to the party?' she asked.

'Let me think,' said Alex. 'Let's see. How about that nightdress my mother gave you for Christmas?'

'Alex! I can't wear a nightdress to a party!'

'You can to this one, sweetheart. It's a very special party. Just the two of us in the dining-room in ten minutes' time. Now, don't come till I call you.'

Exactly ten minutes later, Judy heard Alex shout, 'Ready!' and she gave herself a final check in the mirror. She had brushed out her chestnut curls until they shone, and when she moved a faint scent of Arpège drifted through the air. The nightdress looked stunning, a filmy green froth of silk and lace, displaying a daring swoop of cleavage. She smiled at herself in the mirror and her eyes sparkled. Dear Alex!

Whatever did he have in mind?

She found out when she walked into the dining-room a moment later. Alex must have moved at the speed of light, for not only had he changed into a smartly tailored dressing-gown himself, but he had also transformed the room. The Tiffany lampshade cast a rose-pink glow over a table exquisitely set for two.

'Happy anniversary, darling,' said Alex, taking her in his arms.

'Anniversary?' asked Judy wonderingly, feeling his heart thudding through the corduroy dressing-gown.

'Yes,' said Alex. 'It's the fifth anniversary of our first time together. Or had you forgotten?'

'No, I hadn't,' whispered Judy. 'But I thought you would have.'

'Well, it was lucky it was New Year's Eve,' confessed Alex. 'It's an easy date to remember. Now, just a minute, I want to get this right.'

He moved across to the record player and let the arm down gently. To her astonishment, Judy heard a scratched but still vigorous recording of Vera Lynn spring to life, singing 'We'll Meet Again.' She swallowed the lump in her throat and turned to admire the table. Alex had thought of everything. There was the best lace tablecloth, the Sèvres china, French crystal, champagne chilling in an ice-bucket, and two plates of smoked salmon delicately garnished with chervil and lemon. And in the centre of the table was the finishing touch. A crystal vase containing five long-stemmed red carnations.

Judy's eyes misted over and she felt for Alex's hand and squeezed it wordlessly.

'Is it all right?' he asked anxiously. 'I wanted it to be perfect.'

'It is,' said Judy joyfully. 'Absolutely perfect.'

2 NEW TITLES
FOR MARCH 1990

Jo *by Tracy Hughes.*
Book two in the sensational quartet of sisters in search of love…

In her latest cause, Jo's fiery nature helps her as an idealistic campaigner against the corrupting influence of the rock music industry. Until she meets the industry's heartbreaker, E. Z. Ellis, whose lyrics force her to think twice.   £2.99

Sally Bradford's debut novel **The Arrangement** is a poignant romance that will appeal to readers everywhere.

Lawyer, Juliet Cavanagh, wanted a child, but not the complications of a marriage. Brady Talcott answered her advertisement for a prospective father, but he had conditions of his own…   £2.99

W✸RLDWIDE

Medical Romance

DISCOVER THE THRILL
OF 4 EXCITING MEDICAL
ROMANCES — FREE!

FREE BOOKS FOR YOU

In the exciting world of modern medicine, the emotions of true love have an added drama. Now you can experience **FREE** four of these unforgettably romantic tales of passion and heartbreak - and look forward to a regular supply of Mills & Boon Medical Romances delivered to your door!

Turn the page for details of 2 extra free gifts, and how to apply.

AN IRRESISTIBLE OFFER
FROM MILLS & BOON

Here's an offer from Mills & Boon to become a regular reader of Medical Romances. To welcome you, we'd like you to have four books, an enchanting pair of glass oyster dishes and a special MYSTERY GIFT.

Then, every two months you could look forward to receiving 6 more brand new Medical romances for £1.35 each, delivered direct to your door, post and packing **free**. Plus our newsletter featuring author news, competitions and special offers.

This invitation comes with no strings attached. You can cancel or suspend your subscription at any time, and still keep your **free** books and gifts.

It's so easy. Send no money now. Simply fill in the coupon below at once and post it to-

Reader Service, FREEPOST, PO Box 236, Croydon, Surrey CR9 9EL

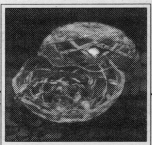

- -

YES! Please rush me my 4 Free Medical Romances and 2 FREE gifts!

Please also reserve me a Reader Service Subscription. If I decide to subscribe, I can look forward to receiving 6 brand - new Medical Romances, every two months, for just **£8.10**, delivered direct to my door. Post and packing is **free**. If I choose not to subscribe I shall write within 10 days - I can keep the books and gifts whatever I decide. I can cancel or suspend my subscription at any time, I am over 18 years of age.   **EP75D**

NAME _____

ADDRESS _____

_____

_____ *POSTCODE* _____

SIGNATURE _____

MAILING PREFERENCE SERVICE